True

True

A Contemporary Retelling of Rahab

S.E. CLANCY

ISBN -13-978-1-7335195-0-2

Origami Crickets Publications

For Michael and my girls.

Chapter 1

"Put the money on the nightstand."

True kept her back to the man when she sat up on the edge of the bed, toes flexing on the cold floor. She shrugged on her silk robe and stood, tying the sash, as her client fumbled with his pants. "Take your time," she said, padding toward the pristine granite and stainless steel kitchen, glancing at the digital clock to check his appointment length. "I will get you a drink."

He seemed like the whiskey type, so she poured a finger into a tumbler. Across the room, the young man sped through the buttons on his shirt, nervously smiling when he saw her watching. "Sorry," he mumbled, jamming the tails into the waist of his designer trousers.

"No need for that. I apologize if I made you feel rushed."

"I should get back to the office, anyways. My boss is breathing down my neck for the border reports."

True stepped around the counter and retrieved his tie from the floor. She snaked the blue fabric around his collar and waited until he stilled to begin tying the knot. "It must be awful for you, with the enemy's army a day or two away."

He cleared his throat, looking anywhere but her eyes. "Yeah, a bit nerve-wracking since they rolled over two countries in three months."

"And we are next."

"Looks like it." He grabbed his coat from the chair. "But I shouldn't be talking with you about it."

She helped him settle the jacket onto his shoulders and turned him to work the buttons. Easing a smile across her face, True reached up and straightened his hair. "My job is to make you forget, even if for an hour. What you say or do stays in this room."

"Yeah, Henry said that, too."

True hummed, and handed him the whiskey, which he knocked back.

"Can I see you again this week?"

"I will send you a text."

"What if I can't make that time?"

She placed her manicured hand on his cheek and raised one eyebrow. The innocence of first-timers always softened her heart a bit. "I'll send you a few options."

He thanked her no less than three times before closing the door. True flicked on the doorway cameras and watched him trot down the sidewalk.

After tucking the money into the safe hidden under a bathroom drawer, she changed the linens and reassembled her room before heading to the shower. There was a long three-hour break and she meant to use every minute of it.

Escaping through the opening next to the kitchen, True tucked her wet hair into a braid and climbed the stairs to her personal apartment. She slipped through another door and into the heavy overalls and leather apron from the peg next to the door. Metal filings covered the floor. She decided not to sweep until she was done. There were eighty-three more tubes to cut and grind. Then, it was on to assembly.

When her alarm sounded, she was only halfway through. Still, she gathered the materials and headed to the roof. The breeze pushed her sculptures into motion, spinning and reflecting the fading sunlight. True deposited the tubes into a pile, each engraved with a number. Soon, they would sing every time the wind blew.

The sun dipped behind the mountain range to the west. True looked north, squinting to try and see the invader's camp. Pinprick lights blinked on beyond the river. Only twenty miles of flat farmlands separated them from the capital city, perched on the hill and surrounded by sheer cliffs. It was unsettling—their previous conquests leveled entire cities from that distance or more. Her house precariously settled inches from the drop-off. Only a few brave men, confronted with their wives banging on the front door, had used her flimsy rope ladder, that lay heaped at the bottom of her rusted red fire escape, to escape down the unclimbable cliff face.

Her second alarm sounded. Ten minutes until General Kohl came for his daily visit. True hustled downstairs, fastening the roof hatch behind her. Clean-up would have to wait and she shucked her apron to the floor and pulled on a shimmering robe.

She'd barely dusted her sweat with talc powder and spritzed on the perfume he preferred, when his two-rapped knock sounded at her door. Pulling open the door, True smiled wide. "Jared."

"I tried to find your last name again," he said, pushing into her body. "I'll find you out one day."

"A girl has her secrets." And she knew he'd never find her past. She spent her first earnings burying and burning any trace connecting her to the family across town, or the dilapidated house she'd shared with her siblings. No, Jared Kohl would never link True to her drunkard father, who was wasting away from cancer. They'd never even seen her beautiful home built on the city cliffs, fortified deep into the bedrock.

Jared buried his lips into her neck, stripping away her robe, all work and no play. "Never underestimate me."

"I never have," she said, stepping backwards to the bed. "That's why you're still allowed to come."

"Less talk."

By the time she redressed, Jared snored deeply. True sautéed chicken and vegetables until he stirred. She poured two glasses of wine and plated dinner as he sat on the stool at the counter.

"It's really good," he mumbled between bites.

"I thought I'd try something new. You need more variety in your diet."

"I like meat."

"I know." She sipped her wine and used a nearby remote to close her blinds. "I saw the army earlier, just over the river."

Jared's fork paused near his mouth. "Yeah. The President's sure they won't be able to make it past the defenses."

"He's certainly confident, given their reputation to crush everything in their path." Any city that'd put up a fight was burned to the ground. The news had no shortage of first-hand footage.

"Well, the President's my boss, so I do what he tells me to do." He scraped the fork against the plate. "Got any more?"

True served him the last of the stir fry and rinsed her dish. "How many days until they arrive?"

She dried her plate slowly, as if it would delay the army.

"We're sending out an envoy tomorrow, to see if there's any negotiating."

"Are you going?"

Jared snorted. "I'm not that stupid. The last place that tried had their guy's dog tags sent back. Nothing else."

"That's awful." She glanced to the covered windows. "Though it's brilliant psychological warfare."

"And what do you know about that?"

" 'The supreme art of war is to subdue the enemy without fighting.' "

"What's that? Something you read?" He jerked his head to her small immaculate bookcase. He had no idea about the one a story above, stretching floor to ceiling, books jammed into every space.

True retrieved his plate and dipped it into the suds. "It's Sun Tzu."

"Sun who?" He belched and gulped down the last of his wine.

"Sun Tzu. He wrote 'The Art of War.' "

"Never heard of it."

She kept her eyes on the dish. "He was a Chinese military strategist and writer."

Jared retreated back to the bed and dressed. "Didn't know you were so interested in war."

Refilling his wine, she trailed him and set the glass on the nightstand. "Not war, but in things that are interesting to you. After all, I have to keep you captivated." Though she wanted to strip the bed and start a load of laundry, True buttoned Jared's light green work shirt.

He wrapped his soft fingers around her waist. "It's not your brain that interests me."

"Oh? It must be my cooking." Her fingers worked toward the collar.

"No. It's not even the wine."

She patted his chest when he nibbled her shoulder through the expensive robe. "Ah, ah," she said, pulling back. "None of that, General Kohl. You know the rules."

Jared swore. He reached into his pocket and tossed a wad of cash onto her nightstand. "You and your rules."

"Without rules, there is anarchy."

"Sun Tzu?"

"No. Me."

He sat to tie his shoes. "Ah, my mysterious True with no last name. Maybe I'll call in a favor to the justice center."

True plodded toward the door. She stopped and looked over her shoulder with a practiced smile. "Idle threats."

"No vegetables tomorrow, or I'll do it."

She laughed politely and opened the door. The smile disappeared the moment the lock clicked into place. Skipping his departure on the cameras, True cleaned up and showered again. She slipped into some soft pants and a tank top.

Once back inside her workshop with the television news turned on, she swept the metal shavings into a pile while the broadcasters showed the latest footage. The enemy's weapons were more superior than the ones Jared bragged his army had. Even long-range camera shots couldn't hide their infantry numbers. She turned the television off.

The city didn't have a chance.

True recycled the filings into a pot to melt. While she worked on the last tubes, she tried not to think about what would happen if the President decided to fight. Instead, she played through scenarios following the city's concession. With no soldiers to pay her way, since they'd surely be pressed into service or jailed, True would be left with her art. She could go to the store without worrying about bumping into a client's wife, or having someone mutter, "Slut," as she passed.

But then again, she was quite sure she could fall back on the business she'd built up. Even though the army was rumored to hold to religious, high moral standards, there had to be some in the bunch who craved a woman after a three year-long deployment.

She trudged up the stairs to the roof hatch, trading the smell of singed metal for the damp Delta breeze, cooling off the flat roof of her home. She'd bought the abandoned home because of the view, without a thought of the aging mortar and bricks. Over the last few years, it became her favorite place in the world, as she learned to craft with metal. Solar lights reflected against the sculptures the spinners twisting next to metal flaps waving from their pegs on a squatted box. The movements reminded her of crows gliding on windy days.

Turning her attention to the towering spindles that looked like a naked, metal tree, True stood on her tiptoes to fit the first tube onto the branch. She worked her way across the sculpture, a smile erupting when the fifth tube finally caught the wind and sang. The sixth and seventh hummed in slightly different tones, their sorrowful melody growing and fading depending on the strength of the wind.

Her screwdriver slipped while she was tightening down another branch and True sliced her palm against the metal. She hissed and dropped the screwdriver to apply pressure. Abandoning the project, she retreated to her workshop and bandaged her hand, using the first aid kit near the welder. There'd been plenty of times she used the burn ointment and gauze.

Forced to halt her song tree sculpture, True plucked a book from her upstairs shelves and settled onto an over-stuffed chair near her single bed covered with a well-used comforter and a red blanket folded near the end. For once, her favorite book couldn't hold her attention. She dimmed the lights and opened the blinds. Across the valley, the lights burned bright at the army's camp. From her window, they almost looked closer than they'd been the day before.

She cranked the window open and pressed her forehead into the screen. She cradled her wounded hand against her chest, drawing in the sweet smell of jasmine that drifted on the air from the tendrils that clung to the building.

It reminded True of the plant below her mom's kitchen window, with the tiny pink flowers they'd weave into her sister's braids while they dreamed about graduating school and moving out. Maybe they'd get married and become mothers.

Those dreams died years before.

A pounding on the door below made True slam her hand on the window frame and stinging pain zipped up her arm. No one had made an appointment. She walked down to the monitors near the door and watched the man sway on his feet before placing a hand on the wall to steady himself. He battered on the steel again.

"Can I help you?" True used the intercom she had installed to keep the drunks away.

The man leaned into the peephole, as if it were the microphone. "Jared said ... Jared sent me."

"I'm sorry, but I am not able to see you right now. If you leave a card, I can contact you."

"No, I need to come in now." He banged his fist on the door.

"I do apologize, but you'll need to leave before I call the patrol."

"I am the patrol." A clumsy hand shoved a badge at the peephole and it scraped into the metal.

"Please, leave me your card and we can work something out."

His foot met the kickplate several times. "Let me in. I have money."

True sighed and sent a message to the city patrolmen. Sure, this one would be embarrassed, but it wouldn't be the first time she'd called coworkers to lead away one of their own. "It doesn't work that way."

He snarled insults into the night. She watched as he paced, then stumbled across the street. A couple of his colleagues arrived and guided him down the sidewalk.

With a yawn, True went back upstairs and curled onto the small bed to sleep, pulling the soft red blanket over her clothes. The jasmine wandered through her memories until she drifted off.

When someone pounded on the door again, True was sure the drunk was back. Cracking her eyelids open, sunlight marched in through the open window and directly into her eyes. The second thumping was more insistent as she descended. She swept her hair into a bun when she saw Jared on the monitors.

"General Kohl," she said, opening the door. "Is everything all right?"

"No." He shoved past her and stomped straight to the window. "Their army isn't advancing, and they fired warning shots when our ambassadors approached."

"Oh my." Her practiced words covered the panic in her mind. Without some type of negotiations, they wouldn't survive. Everything she'd worked for would be for nothing.

"The city will be put into curfew before dark. There will be a patrol checkpoint on the road in and no one gets in or out." Jared closed the window and clicked the remote to close the curtains. "So, I won't be by later. Keep your monitors on. Rumor has it that they will try and send in spies to scope out our defenses."

"Will you be safe?"

His eyes closed and he scrubbed the thin hair just above his wrinkled forehead. "I'll be next to the President, trying to figure out how to make it out of this. You have enough food?"

It was the first time Jared had offered kindness rather than money.

"I do, thank you."

"Keep your door bolted and call me if someone shows up."

True nodded.

"Here." He reached into his pocket and pressed some bills into her hand. "Don't let anyone in."

She barely tipped her lips up and nodded again, feeling as cheap as the unsolicited, rumpled money in her fist. The lock slid into place and she dropped the payment near the door.

In her workroom, True turned on quiet music. She knew the radio and television would be blasting panic and simultaneous presidential rhetoric, neither of which she wanted to hear. After a couple hours of cleaning and rearranging materials, True returned to her rooftop project.

She felt like a vampire in the sun with the normal evening hours she kept for clients, but worked in a wide sunhat and gloves. When her arms felt floppy from placing the tubes in a cascading, circular pattern, she stood and stretched. Her body ached more than it should for her age. Her stomach rumbled. The wind sang through the different tubes, all around the hollow trunk as she fastened the roof hatch.

After eating a granola bar over the sink, True popped a couple of aspirin and slathered lotion on her angry, pink sunburn. Clients paid for smooth skin, not peeling blotches. She retrieved the book from the night before and slid onto the cool tiled floor near the kitchen to soothe her skin. Mr. Darcy had snubbed Elizabeth Bennet when a quiet knock came at her door.

Through the monitors, two men looked down the nearly empty street, then whispered to one another. Their skin was dark from the sun and their pants too clean and new. One knocked softly again, before quietly asking, "Hello?" The tourist caps emblazoned with a city name a few hours north were slung low across their eyes. The city had been razed weeks before.

The hairs on the back of True's neck pricked.

These were the spies.

She pulled her phone from her pocket and brought up Jared's number. Something brushed against her bare foot— Jared's cash. Rumpled singles that he probably used for some seedy club across town with the boys.

True twisted the lock and opened the door. "Please, come in before you are seen."

Chapter 2

The two men slid through the door, guns up as they advanced. True steadied her hand against the bolt when she turned the handle. Crouching, she swiped the money into a pocket. She stood and cleared her throat before turning to face them.

Both stood sideways, each with a clear view of the door and window. One had white hair shaved close at the base of his neck and kept his weapon at eye-level. His face was pinched, eyes flicking from the bed to the kitchen to the bookshelf.

The other, closer to her own age, lowered his gun and double-checked the door bolt was in place. His single black braid disappeared into the collar of his black shirt. He noticed her watching and nodded slightly. "Thank you."

"You're welcome." True moved slowly to the kitchen, keeping her hands at her side for the benefit of the older soldier. "Can I get you something to drink?"

"No."

"Yes."

Both men answered at the same time, then glared at one another. Without breaking eye contact, the younger one repeated, "Yes."

True kept her eyes on the task, filling each glass with ice, then filtered water. She approached the older man first, who'd moved to the window and looked toward his comrades. "Can I get you anything to eat?"

Keeping his gun against his thigh, the soldier accepted the water. "No," he said, voice as harsh as a rasp on raw metal.

"I will eat it first," she said, "so that you can see that it's not poisoned."

He placed the glass on the window ledge. After some fishing in a hidden pocket in his pants, he showed her a wrapped bar. "MRE."

She smiled. "I'm sure I can make something a bit tastier."

"I'm good."

True returned to the kitchen counter, sliding the second glass to the younger man who promptly drank the entire thing. "And how about you? Do you also prefer your meals shaped like a brick?"

"No, ma'am. I'll take a home-cooked meal any day." His eyes crinkled at the corners when he smiled.

"I'll get to work, then."

She prepared the meal she'd planned for Jared and divided it onto two plates. The first, she handed to the soldier who sat at the counter. When she tried to offer the remainder to the man at the window, he tore open the MRE and bit off a corner, chewing thoroughly. True retreated to the kitchen and ate the meal opposite of the younger soldier.

"Thank you," the younger man said between bites, mopping up the bits with a roll. He smiled when he saw her watching. "This is good."

"You're welcome."

The man at the window grunted. True looked to him, but he stared out to his army's spotlights. There were news stories of those famous lights, always a shining over their camps at night.

"That's Major Conley. I'm Holoke."

She turned back to the man at the kitchen counter, whose hand was extended.

"True."

"Pleased to meet you, True." His hand was calloused and rough, working hands. "Thanks for letting us in. We'd heard about you and hoped we could ... buy a night." Holoke's last words were choppy and uneven.

"I understand."

"I'm sorry if that offended you." The soldier paused. "It was strictly a tactical reason."

True placed her plate into the sink. "It would take far more than that to offend me. It is what it is."

Conley's phone chirped. He snapped it open and barked into the mouthpiece. His body stilled until he turned to Holoke and True. "I understand."

Before she could ask if everything was all right, True's phone vibrated in her pocket. It was Jared.

"Where are you?" He puffed into the phone like he was running.

True turned away from Holoke. "At home," she mumbled. "Where else would I be?"

"I'm en route." He panted into the phone, feet thumping.

"Jared, what's wrong?" She turned and held a finger to her lips, nodding at Holoke, then crooking her finger to have Conley move closer. True pressed the speaker button on her phone.

"There were two men seen near your house, probably the spies I called about earlier." Jared heaved for breath. "I'm getting together a squad. We'll be there in eight minutes. Do *not* answer the door, whatever you do."

"Oh, I won't."

"Keep your cameras rolling. I want to check the footage."

True disconnected the call. The three sat in silence.

"Were the cameras on when we came?" Conley stepped closer, shoulders squared, glaring at her.

She smiled wide. "Not at all." Stepping to the bank of small monitors, she clicked in a few keystrokes. "Now they are." Red lights blinked at each corner. "Voilà."

"Seven minutes," Holoke said.

"Follow me." True barged into her workshop, and to the hidden hatch. There was only one place no one would look—no one would know about.

The solar lights threw shadows around the rooftop and the men were on True's heels. She slipped open some latches on the short box covered with metal squares, waving in the breeze. "You," she said, pointing at Conley. "Get in." He crouched into the small space and she shoved the box closed.

Moving onto the singing tree, True pulled Holoke by the hand. "You'll need to climb up and get inside."

He swung a leg onto the first branch. The metal groaned and he hesitated.

"Go," she whispered, even though there was no way anyone could hear them. "It's steel, it'll hold."

The tubes sang in the wind until Holoke's dark head disappeared into the hollow trunk. Muffled footsteps echoed in the roadway below and True fled back down, pausing only to lock the hatch. She'd barely closed the workroom door when the pounding on the door made her jump.

She quickly wiped the sweat from her lip and forehead and dried her hands on her pants. Jared was yelling into the intercom.

"I'm sorry," True said, opening the door wide. "I was so scared that I didn't want to open for anyone."

Jared shoved past her, his soldiers in quick succession. She recognized a few faces and kept a nervous smile in place, then switched to blowing small breaths through her pursed lips. They were in full body armor, with helmets, and carried huge, black military guns.

"Presidential warrant," the last soldier said, thrusting a paper into True's hands. "Do not make any attempt to impede our search."

The men seeped into every corner of her lower room, opening every drawer and door. She heard the bathroom shower door open, followed by, "Clear." The entire squad moved upstairs, True following. Jared lowered his weapon and stood next to her when they entered her workroom.

"What's in there?" Jared's breath came in jagged wheezes.

"There is so much extra space in the house that I thought I'd try my hand at art. Painting wasn't much fun, so I moved onto metal."

"Really? What'd you make?"

True gave a practiced laugh and laid her bandaged hand on his arm, barely above the gun. "I just started. I'm happy not to burn myself right now." She squeezed the warrant tightly in her other fist.

A chorus of clear calls sounded and the soldiers lowered their weapons. One climbed the stairs to the roof hatch and gave it a tug before coming back down. They milled around the windows overlooking the valley, looking at the spotlight. Jared ordered his men to assemble and leave.

Once they'd filed outside, he closed the front door and turned to her. "I've never been upstairs before." He laid his gun on the kitchen counter and grabbed True by the waist.

"That's off limits."

"Not for me."

"For anyone but me."

His bottom lip jutted out. "You wound me. I've been faithful to you for years now."

"And you go home to your wife and children every night."

Jared took in a deep breath and released it through his nostrils. "You never miss a detail."

True shimmied her shoulders a bit. "I try not to."

He reached behind her to retrieve his gun and paused, hand mid-air. She turned to see what he was looking at. Holoke's dish was in the sink and hers was on the counter.

"Who was here?" He growled and twisted her back to face him, keeping his hands on her arms.

"Well," she said, "you usually come around now. When you called the first time, I'd put dinner on the plates to keep warm in the oven." The lies spilled with proficient ease.

"We had someone call and say the two men came to your house."

"Jared, you're hurting me."

He dropped his hands, leaving red finger marks on her bare skin. "Well, did you see them?"

"Yes, but I ..."

"What?" Jared yelled, spittle hitting True's face.

"Please, let me finish," she said, lowering her voice.

His radio crackled to life. "General, you code-four?"

Jared's nostrils flared. "Affirmative." His jaw worked. He jerked his chin up at True. "Explain."

"Right before you called the second time, there were two men at my door. They were pounding and wouldn't stop."

"Why didn't you tell me on the phone?"

"You were running, so I figured you'd catch them on the way here."

He swore at her and hauled her by one arm to the door. Jared yanked the door open and thrust her into the street. "Two men stopped by right before we got here." He addressed the soldiers and then glared at True. "Describe them."

"Um, one had a limp. I could see it as they ran away. They had on dirty pants and hats, but one had long blonde hair." She shuddered for effect. "The other had a handgun." Too many false details and they'd catch on.

"Which way did they go?"

"Towards the main road out. The limping one really falling behind, so if you hurry, you guys might actually catch him."

Jared remained behind while his men ran down the sidewalk, their uniforms disappearing into the shadows beyond the streetlights, shouting into their lapel radios. "My jeep is coming."

True nudged his shoulder with hers. "I'm sorry I didn't tell you before. I was out of sorts when the one guy gave me the warrant." She smoothed the crumpled paper. "I've only ever heard of these."

"Yeah, well, you have a pretty powerful guy in your bed."

She slowly folded the warrant into even squares, gauging her next response. General Kohl didn't reach his status by being a pawn. He was a political chess master with a penchant for a pretty face.

"That's why I'm trying to get you to eat more vegetables."

His laughter echoed into the night. When headlights rounded the corner, he swallowed hard and his face turned stern. Wordless, he climbed into the armored vehicle and it rumbled off in the same direction as his men.

A cool breeze made True shiver. She went inside her home, slid the bolt into place, and turned off the recording. The plate on the counter might as well have a spotlight shining on it. How could she be so careless? Traitors were treated to old-fashioned justice: stripped naked, branded, and paraded through the city before their house was set on fire. The President loved drama and the people clamored for his heavy-handed flare.

Once the dishes were washed and put away, True splayed her hands on the counter. Holoke and Conley still had to get out unseen. Her house would probably have extra patrols. And worst of all, she still had no idea why she'd let them in—other than an overwhelming feeling it was the right thing to do.

True double-checked the monitors before going upstairs. She turned on some lights and others off so that, from the outside, it looked like any other evening. Tugging on a sweater, she paused at the rooftop hatch. Maybe they would take her with them so she could start over again, without a reputation. She'd work as a janitor if she had to.

The hatch silently swung open, True grateful she'd greased it earlier in the year. From the roof's ledge, she could see the headlights leave the city, next to bouncing flashlights. Gravel crunched inside of the box where Conley hid.

"They've gone," she said, crouching to release him from his prison.

He groaned and pressed his legs flat. A soft thump made True turn as Holoke straightened from his jump, grimacing. "Ow," he whispered. "I'm getting old." He limped forward and offered a hand to Conley.

"You can see them from here," True said, standing at the roof wall once more. She pointed to the headlights.

"How many were there?" Conley brought up binoculars.

"Twelve, I believe."

He squinted into the lenses. "What'd you tell them?"

"That one of you had a limp and a gun and the other had long blonde hair."

"Thank you." Holoke leaned against the wall near her left elbow. "Nice view."

"It was the reason I bought the house. No one wanted a stack of crumbling bricks with drafty windows, built on the cliffside of the city." She smiled into the darkness. "But who could argue with this?"

The younger soldier leaned over the short wall. "And a fire escape! I'm pretty sure only someone with a death wish would take that route."

True pointed down. "There's a rope ladder down there that drops down to an old goat path that hang gliders use. It's only been used twice, since some wives were not too keen to hear their husbands were here."

Conley's phone screen lit up. He pounced his fingers across the screen. "We have to wait for a signal before we leave, in case they double back."

"Let's go inside," True said. "They may send up aircraft."

She led them back through her workshop and the bedroom area.

Holoke stopped in the middle of the second room as True was starting down the stairs. "Why is there a bed up here, too?"

"This is my home. Downstairs is my work."

Conley pushed past Holoke and then True, boots clomping against the wood until he hit the floor below. Holoke looked around. "Makes sense. It's nicer up here."

True looked at her tattered bedspread, something she'd bought because it reminded her of the one she had when she was a little girl. Before everything changed. "No one is supposed to see this except for me." Her eyes flicked to the overstuffed bookcases and funky green curtains that were almost ugly if they weren't perfect.

"Why did you let us in?"

She leaned back against the wall. "That's the million-dollar question." Her eyes closed and she tilted her head back. "I wish I could say instinct. Or karma. Or whatever you believe in. But, I knew I had to open the door." The money in her pocket poked her thigh. She peered at Holoke.

The twitch near Holoke's mouth was barely noticeable, but she made a living finding those tics. True plucked a book from the massive shelves. "Centuries ago, Queen Sheba heard of Solomon's wisdom. She didn't believe in the same God, but Solomon's reputation drew her. She instinctively knew that he had the answers she needed." She flipped the book over in her hands. "I just knew I had to open the door. There wasn't a question in my mind."

"I'm glad you did." Holoke eased himself into her favorite chair.

"I grew up hearing about you—well your people. Who didn't? An entire country who'd lost a war, became enslaved for decades, and then broke free."

"That was my grandparents."

"Well, your parents must've been the ones helping start up the army advance to take back what is rightfully yours."

"Rightfully ours?"

True slid down the wall to the top stair. "Look. I don't know everything, but I do know that your people worship a god—"

Holoke interrupted. "No, it's God. Big G." He smiled, teeth showing, hands resting on his legs.

She tilted her head in acknowledgement. "Okay, God. He must be a pretty powerful God to allow you to defeat city after city."

He nodded, one eyebrow up.

"There is no way this city will stand in your way. And … and I want a promise from you."

"I don't make the rules. I'm not that high up the food chain."

"I trust that you'll try."

Holoke leaned forward. "What kind of promise?"

Chapter 3

"We don't negotiate." Conley stood at the bottom of the staircase, his palm resting on his holstered pistol, his voice loud enough for Holoke to hear.

"I'm not negotiating," True said, twisting to face the older man. "I'm asking for assistance since I helped you. I could've easily shown them where you were."

Conley grunted and turned away.

True watched him scrutinize her business area. He was the stoic type who'd probably never set foot in a prostitute's house until they'd crossed her threshold. Conley turned to stare at her, and slightly set his bottom jaw forward, refusing to return her smile.

Behind her, Holoke shifted. She looked and he was leaning closer to her bed, touching the fraying patches. "Reminds me of something my mom had."

"Me too," she replied quietly. She would sleep on her side on the edge of the bed, to keep her sister from tumbling onto the floor during the night. It'd taken her years to get used to a pillow. "I want to keep my family safe." She turned back to Conley. "Could you do that? Allow me and my family to live?"

The seasoned soldier stepped away from the stairs and out of sight.

She stared at Holoke, clamping her teeth together. "Certainly, your God would allow that."

Holoke found the bedspread so interesting that he didn't look up.

True inhaled, ready to plead again, but stopped short. "You introduced him as Major, but you did not give your rank."

He smiled at the floor. "Guilty." He glanced at his watch and finally looked at True. "Colonel Manaba Holoke."

"That's a mouthful."

"Luckily, most people don't have to spell it."

She lowered her voice and glanced down to the empty area. "Is there a problem that you outrank Conley, then?"

"Not at all. He joined later in life. I was practically born into the service."

"Then why does he hate me?"

The Colonel cleared his throat. "He is a soldier and committed to finishing his assignment. We didn't plan on getting trapped in the city."

"So, you can make the decision about sparing my family?"

"I can."

True stood and straightened her shirt before approaching the bed and sitting within reach of Holoke's chapped hand. "Do you need something in exchange?"

"No!" The armchair groaned against the floor as he stood and propelled himself backwards. "I mean, no, it's not like that. Not at all."

She swallowed hard. "Please, let me save my family," she whispered, not even sure why she asked for the lives of those who had ignored her for years.

"He's right," Holoke said, grasping the back of his neck. "We've never negotiated."

True pulled her shoulders back and blinked quickly to clear her eyes. "I understand." She would pack lightly, and leave as soon as they set off, even if she had to walk to the nearest town. She'd probably starve first, but it'd be better than waiting like a caged animal.

"But, I'm not so cold to see what you did for us." Holoke lowered himself back into the chair, out of her reach. "Major!"

"Sir!" Conley's feet ascended until his cropped hair came into view.

"You are correct. We do not negotiate. But, we are not immune to mercy, nor to terms of forfeit."

She methodically placed her hands in her lap, keeping her eyes on the Colonel. True's shoulders ached from holding them so straight and the anticipation was worse than the day she hid behind her father's desk, when he suggested she do housework for the loan shark who'd come to collect debts.

Holoke pulled his braid from beneath the neckline of the body armor. "If you swear to God, the same one who has allowed us to defeat those in our way, that you won't tell anyone we were here or when we left, we will honor your promise to allow anyone in your house to live."

"Sir!" Conley's tone made True flinch. "You cannot break protocol for ... a pretty face."

Holoke looked past her shoulder, jaw muscles flexing. "Major, at ease. I will deal with this personally."

"Thank you," she breathed, tears pricking her eyes again.

"Only family who are actually in your house on the day this city is seized."

"Yes, of course. Thank you."

"Major, sweep the first floor and make sure it's secure. We should rest until we get the signal."

"Yes, sir." Behind her, the stairs creaked as Conley descended.

True's phone vibrated. "The city is on lockdown. No one in or out," she read out loud.

"May I sleep in this chair?" Holoke righted the armchair and slumped down, his head leaning back.

"Do you want a blanket?"

"No. The layers keep me warm."

He slid the gun from his holster and placed it across his lap, fingers wrapped around the grip, and trigger finger resting alongside the barrel. His eyelids lowered and soon, his breathing fell even.

She glided down the stairs, careful to avoid the boards she knew would squeak. Conley had shut the window and was looking at how to close the blinds. True used the clicker and smiled when he turned.

"The couch is pretty comfortable. Would you like a blanket?"

"No." He gave the couch a side-eye, as if it would infect him with some foreign disease. "Can you turn on those cameras?"

"Of course." She powered on the monitors. "Would you like me to record?"

"Negative."

Conley sat on the edge of the couch's expensive material before lying flat, his head where he could see the door. He mirrored his commander's posture, pistol across his thigh.

True perched on one of the lower stairs, back against the cool bricks. She was cold but didn't dare move for a blanket. Instead, she watched the camera screens as moths and bugs crowded the street lights. Once, a person streaked by so fast, she couldn't tell if it was a man or woman.

Somewhere after midnight, Conley jerked awake. His head swiveled until he saw True. As he sat up, he holstered his weapon and retrieved his buzzing phone.

"Is it time?" she whispered. "I'll go wake the Colonel."

The only people who'd stepped foot into her private loft were the men who'd delivered the bed and chair years ago—other than Jared's troop some hours before. True paused at the top step at the sight of Holoke asleep in the chair. His mouth was closed, eyebrows relaxed. Tiny muscles flinched near his mouth. In another place, a different lifetime, she might have pursued the handsome soldier who'd given her the promise of a lifetime.

She'd never had to wake an armed man before. True made a wide path and approached him from the side. She gently cleared her throat. "Colonel Holoke," she whispered. "Conley has received your signal to leave."

His eyes rolled forward. Holoke took in a quick, deep breath and looked around. He smiled, eyes puffy, when he saw her. "Thank you."

"Of course. I think he's waiting downstairs."

Holoke stretched and groaned before heading down to his officer. True watched from the kitchen while they quietly discussed their options to get out of the city.

"I can help," she said.

Conley's head angled up from his phone, eyes narrowed.

"The fire escape."

"Lead the way," Holoke said, walking to shadow her path.

Again, the men followed her to the roof. The solar lights were dimmer than before, and the breeze gone. The singing tree barely hummed. Across the open fields, their camp spotlights soared into the blackness, like a pillar of fire.

True leaned over the ledge. "It's old," she murmured. "But, it's anchored in the walls. And I've never had two men use it at once, so I'm not sure how it'll hold."

Conley hopped onto the metal. His boots echoed and they all froze.

"The rope ladder is at the bottom." True pointed to the heap of rope and metal rungs. "It stops just short of the old goat path in the cliff. You'll have a little drop at the bottom."

The soldier curtly nodded and crept down the fire escape, stalling each time it groaned into the night.

"Colonel," she said, once Conley's head faded into the night down the cliff. "I don't think you should go straight back to your camp. I know Jared. He'll stay out for a few days looking for you. Or at least his men will."

Holoke's face was barely visible, but he nodded. He moved closer and leaned down. She hadn't realized how tall he was.

"Give me your phone number."

True spoke the numbers, watching as he typed them into his phone and he slid it into a vest pocket.

"Never answer my texts. Ever." His emphasis on the final word borderlined an order.

"How will I know they are from you?"

He glanced over the roof's edge. "You'll figure it out." When he straightened, she smelled his sweat and deodorant. "You have to keep the ladder hanging when we come back. It'll be easier to spot your house. I can't keep my end of our agreement if I don't know which house is yours."

She nodded, shivering.

"And if you don't have everyone inside, even if you aren't here, I can't promise you anything. Nothing. It won't be my fault if you don't hold up your end of the bargain. Got it?"

"Yes. I'll do it."

Holoke looked down into the dark abyss, and True with him. Far below, a flashlight burst twice. "He made it. My turn."

He vanished sooner than Conley, his black hair melting into the night. True remained at her spot, straining to hear each time a rung clinked into the cliff face or the rope creaked—anything other than a thump of a body after a fall. The tubes started to sing behind her as the winds picked up. Just about the time she decided to turn away, she saw the same flashlight signal.

Creeping back below, the lock fastened on the hatch, True pulled out her phone and looked at the last message Jared had sent. Maybe she could divert his attention, so she asked him how the search went.

31

Crossing her bedroom, she turned off the lights and continued downstairs. Once in darkness, her feet stopped in the kitchen.

Everything she'd planned for, learning how to work with metal to start a new life across the globe, it would all end in days. And if she didn't convince her family to come to her home, she'd somehow be responsible for their deaths, even if she wasn't.

True headed into her bathroom and pulled the bottom drawer completely off of its guides. Perfume bottles and hair clips rattled into each other when it landed on the floor. She ignored the overwhelming scent and reached into the dark space to tug out the small fire safe. Her birth certificate, passport, and house title nestled beside the stacks of sorted and rubber-banded money inside the small safe. She carried the entire thing to the canopied downstairs bed and spread the contents across the bedspread. Her hopes for the future laid out in front of her, True crammed the tendrils of panic down to focus on what she needed to do.

All she'd built was strictly for herself, never a family—especially the one she'd been ripped from. The private investigator kept his reports brief over the years. True had six nieces and nephews, ranging from toddlers to teens. Her sister lived with their parents to help care for their sick father. Her brother lived a couple hours away and visited often. They all seemed to be happy. It was easier to know about them instead of interrupting their lives.

Until now.

True repacked the safe and moved it to the kitchen counter. She pulled down the velvet drapes from the bed and stripped the beaded bedspread off, kicking them underneath the mahogany frame. It all seemed so ridiculous as she looked to the shaded window.

"Well, God-with-a-big-G, if you are there, I hope you heard what Colonel Holoke promised me." True squared her shoulders to the empty room and looked to the white-washed ceiling with its fancy mood lighting. "Whatever you want me to promise, I will. I swear I won't even touch another man. Just help me get my family here. Uh, thank you."

Feeling as useful as an ashtray on a motorcycle, True went to her fridge for a snack. She clicked open the curtain on the way and the army's lights stood like soldiers at attention. The spotless shelves in the refrigerator held a few apples and cheese, some salad dressing and packaged bacon. She'd need a lot more food if her family came, and there'd be no time to shop once they'd arrived. True opened a glass-faced cupboard. There weren't even enough dishes for half of them.

She checked the time and tucked a wad of money into her sweatshirt pocket. Maybe it was better to call in the groceries for delivery like she always did, but she didn't even know what to ask for. So, she shuffled out of the front door, and into the dark morning, her fur-lined slippers scuffing along the sidewalk.

"Excuse me," a man called, seconds before True was blinded by a flashlight. "Oh, hey, True."

She shielded her eyes. "Good morning."

"You shouldn't be out. There's a curfew."

"Yes, General Kohl advised me. Could you ...?"

The light lowered from her face.

"I need groceries before everyone loses their minds and clears the shelves." As her sight adjusted to the reflected beam, she recognized the pair of officers. "Sorry I didn't see you before, Gerrick." She nodded to the other man. "Anders."

"True."

"You two drew the short end of the watch stick?" True grinned and tucked her hair behind her ears. It was simple enough to distract them.

Anders drooped, his rifle slung across one shoulder. "It was my anniversary last night, too."

True placed her hand on his. "I'm so sorry, Anders. Did you have plans?" She stepped in the direction of the grocer's, both soldiers falling in line beside her.

"Yeah. We had reservations for dinner and a sitter all lined up for the kids. She went home and said we'll do it some other day."

"You should, Anders."

"Doubt it'll happen with the army being so close."

Her favorite grocery store was still dark inside, but she knew the owner and his teenage son would be opening soon. "Maybe you should whisk her off to some overnight trip?"

"Yeah. Maybe."

"I'll whisk you off on an overnight trip, True." Gerrick's hand snuck to her waist.

She gently smacked it away and smiled. "Only if I allow it."

Anders gulped his snicker into a cough as a light flicked on inside of the store.

Gnarled and hunched over, Mr. Aoki hobbled to the floor. "Coming, coming," he said through the glass. The lock thudded and he pulled the door back. "Please come in."

They all mumbled their thanks and entered. The black-haired teen scrunched his face when he walked into the store from the back room.

"Good morning, Bailey," True said, grabbing a cart. Turning back to the officers, she said, "Thank you for walking me down. I'll let you get back to it." She pushed the cart down the closest aisle and waited for the bell above the door to jingle.

Mr. Aoki straightened some nearby bread. "You didn't call in your order?"

"No. I have family coming over and I need a lot of food."

"Oh. I didn't know you had a big family."

"No one does. I'd appreciate it if you didn't mention it to anyone."

The grocer bobbed his salt and pepper hair. "Of course. Do you need some help?"

True looked at the bread. "Yes. I've never shopped for a lot of people."

"How many?"

"Maybe around eleven?"

Bailey whistled. "That's an entire football team."

True shrugged.

"How many days will they be staying with you?" Mr. Aoki had already put four loaves of bread in the cart.

"Uh, a week?"

The older man chuckled. "Leave it to me. I've got a pack of kids and gobs of in-laws."

"Perfect." Better that she left the decisions to someone with a clue.

True abandoned the cart, pressed cash into Mr. Aoki's hand, and flagged down a passing taxi. She called back to the store to let them know she'd be back home in a couple of hours.

The sun peeked over the mountains to the east, spilling yellow beams onto the tall buildings. The city was waking, ignorant to General Kohl's pursuit of the phantom spies.

But True was far away in her mind after she gave the address to the driver. She was covering bread to let it rise, her small hands working with her mother's. Her sister wiggled when True tried to braid her long, black hair. Their baby brother squalled in his crib. Then, True sat on the steps of the townhouse, plucking the sweet center of the jasmine blooms out to suck on.

When the cab pulled onto the street of her childhood home, her chin wobbled.

The driver flipped around at the end of the road and drove her back home, as soon as she asked.

True turned her key and leaned into her front door. After closing it behind her, she straightened, smoothed her hair, and called for her groceries. It wouldn't do anyone any good to fall apart.

Bailey grinned at the amount of his tip after he lugged it all inside and stored the cold goods into the refrigerator. True caught her reflection in the mirror near the door as she let him out. The dark shadows reflected that she'd nearly been awake for nearly twenty-four hours.

Trudging up the stairs to her room, True plopped onto the bed. She glanced at the chair, still cockeyed after Holoke's departure.

He didn't have to give her the flashlight signal, but it made her fall asleep easier.

Chapter 4

Her dark-haired baby boy slipped from True's arms when her eyes opened. She blinked the dream away, thunder rumbling beyond the window. No infant would ever rest in her arms. The doctors guaranteed that outcome after years of injections. The wisps of longing sank their talons into her heart, so she kicked off the tattered bedspread and sat up.

True padded to the window, stretching out her sore muscles. Once the blackout curtains were pulled aside, cloudy sunlight streamed into the room. Toes splayed on the cool floor, she looked across the valley, where an enormous cloud of steam or smoke billowed above the army's camp. A breeze moved something barely out of view and it clattered against the old brick siding—the rope ladder. Hopefully Holoke and Conley were hunkered down somewhere passing time, because Jared would never give up that easily.

Her stomach reminded her that she needed to eat. The contents in the refrigerator reminded her that she needed to try and get her family to her home. A knock at the door reminded her of the business she ran.

The soldier slunk away when she told him business was closed until the unpleasantries with the army were solved.

She watched the citizens walking down the narrow streets, as if nothing was wrong. It made her shiver, despite the warmth radiating from the sidewalk.

Back inside, True moved and shifted furniture to try and make it seem more inviting to "normal" people. Somehow, she shoved and yanked the bed to the farthest wall and added pillows to make it look more like a lounging couch. Her mom wasn't an idiot, and there was no doubt in True's mind that she knew full well what her oldest did for a living.

Never fully satisfied with her effort, True showered and changed into something comfortable, that wouldn't scream "prostitute" to her father. She called for a driver and soon was on the same route back to her childhood home. A block away, she asked the cab to stop.

How was she supposed to talk her family into coming to her house? They hadn't seen her in over a decade. Certainly, she couldn't waltz up and say, "This is crazy, but I'm here now. You should come move into my house, but I can't tell you why." There wasn't even time to build up a friendship or trust. The army could march up to the cliff at any moment.

Her feet stuck to the pavement while children scrambled about and dogs barked. Down and across the road, she could see the steps she and Elyse played on as girls. True always played with the mother doll and Elyse with the little girl. They'd be girl knights on a quest or Jane Austen characters. And no matter how hard she tried, Elyse could never braid True's hair.

"My fingers won't coolperate."

"Cooperate."

"Coo-oo-perate."

"Co-op-er-ate."

"Dey won't."

As True walked toward her parents' home, there on the same chipped front steps, two small girls in ripped jeans and bright t-shirts lay across the cement, books open and high in the air. Their brown, braided hair spilled down the treads. The screen door to the townhouse needed a new coat of paint, but the jasmine blossoms pulled True closer.

"Hello," she said, crossing the street.

They both turned their heads and True saw Elyse in their freckled stubby noses.

"Is your mom here?"

The older girl lowered her book and sat up. "We don't talk to strangers, lady."

"Yeah," the younger echoed, crawling behind her sister's back.

"You don't know me, but I'm not exactly a stranger. We just haven't met yet."

"Nana!" The older sister stood slowly, eyes staying on True, pulling up the other girl. "There's someone out here!"

"Oh. I'm sorry. I didn't know your grandma was here." True's heart raged against her chest. When footsteps creaked down the hallway behind the screen door, it became hard to breathe.

"Girls?" A shadow darkened the screen. True could recognize that ugly red apron anywhere. Her mother pushed the door open. "Come inside, girls."

June Loyoza looked down from the threshold as the girls scampered by. Her hair was still piled into a twisted bun near her neck, and her silver-rimmed glasses matched the silver throughout her brown hair. She slowly wiped her hands on the bottom edge of the apron. True knew that straight outline in the long pocket was a wooden spoon.

"Hey, Mom." True swallowed hard and gritted her teeth to keep focus. It'd been fourteen years since she'd come home from school and said the same thing, only to be pried from her hiding place a few hours later, never to return until this moment. Should she even still call the woman before her "Mom" or by her first name?

"I never thought you'd come back." Her mom's confession blurted moments before a sob echoed on the building across the street.

True shuffled forward to the bottom step as her mother covered her face and wept. "I didn't think I would either."

"Come inside, come in." June held the screen open and motioned for True, who obeyed. As she passed, her mom touched her elbow.

Automatically turning left once inside the door, True looked at the same living room she'd been forced to leave: same couch, same carpet, same drapes. The only thing that looked remotely new was the television on the wall, mounted on the same wallpaper. She moved beyond her mom and stood near the blue lounger.

"Where's Dad?"

True had been paying a private nurse to come to the house twice a week for the past year, once she found out his prognosis. She didn't ask for reports or updates. She simply paid the bill two months in advance. The bills hadn't stopped, so she knew he hadn't died.

"He's resting in bed." Her mom's eyes dammed with fresh tears.

"I know about the cancer, Mom."

The tears spilled over. "He will be so happy to see you, True."

The ironic part was that Jared would never know she'd used her real name all along.

True kept her response to herself, because a tiny part of her wanted to rage at a man who would trade his own daughter. Over the years, she found that tamping down the truth was better for business than arguing or staring the past in the face. She simply nodded to the furniture. "It really hasn't changed much."

"Can I get you something to drink?"

"No, I'm fine, thank you. Is Elyse here?"

"It's Saturday. She's working at the clinic."

Little feet hammered across the bedroom floor above their heads. "Her girls are beautiful," True said.

June looked at the stained ceiling. "They keep me busy, but they are good girls."

Her words stung True, who'd tried to be a good daughter and get decent grades in school. There'd never been a day she hadn't regretted sneaking out twice to meet the boy down the street. It's no wonder her dad had made the decision to negotiate her away for the debt.

But that was a whole lifetime ago. True exhaled through pursed lips. "Is Dad awake?"

"Let me go check." Her mom zipped through the kitchen, toward the back bedroom. True waited for her mother's foot to hit the squeaky floorboard right outside of their room.

She heard the girls' mumbled chatting overhead and wondered if Elyse had shown them the dark corner of the closet, where it was coolest. On the weekends, they'd use flashlights and read until the batteries died, then make up stories until they were hungry. And if they were very, very lucky, their brother would give up trying to push past the barricade at the door and leave them alone to finish the afternoon reading or drawing on the bare floor, shifting places to soak in the cool spots.

June's muffled voice trickled through the house. True shifted from one foot to the other and her leg brushed against the desk in the corner. There was a different chair. She walked to the back of the desk, a few feet from the wall, and sat down. Without looking, True knew the bills were in the second drawer down on the left, and the top drawer was filled with pens, pencils, and a few scissors. To the right, hanging files with important documents underneath the tape dispenser. And the empty space between the drawers was where her life changed.

The floorboard creaked again. "True?" Her mom whispered and looked around the living room as she entered. Her lips barely crept up when she saw True behind the desk. "Your dad would like to see you."

True's heart banged into her ribs all over again as she trailed her mom through the kitchen, across the cracked linoleum. When her foot hit the noisy patch, she halted.

For so many years, she hated her dad. It was his fault he'd gambled away his paychecks and sent her to a man who'd turned her from an innocent, teenage housekeeper to something much more detestable. She'd waited, like Cinderella, for her prince to save her. In the end, she lived the nightmare until her dragon died one night.

She didn't become a princess. It was too hard to wait for food to suddenly appear.

Finally, True stepped into her parents' bedroom. The curtains, old blankets really, completely blocked the window. A diffuser pumped lavender and peppermint into the cramped space. The only light in the dark, stuffy room came from a small lamp near the doorway.

"The chemo has really affected his hearing and sensitivity to light," June whispered, motioning for True to squeeze in next to her, at the foot of the bed.

Propped against the wall on a mountain of pillows, William Loyoza adjusted his position. White hair bolted in every direction from his head. He finally settled, smoothing the blankets across the lower half of his body with knotted fingers. His crumpled sweatshirt hung like an oversized, empty sack from his shoulders. He took his time, never looking up.

True held her hands together to keep from fiddling. "Hey, Dad."

He finally looked up. His bloodshot eyes, once blue as a spring day, sunken into his skull. "True."

She didn't respond. He was so much smaller than she remembered.

"You came back."

"Yes." True didn't know what else to say.

Instead, she looked at the pictures on the walls, the life they'd lived without her: Elyse's wedding and the babies. Her parents smiling from a beach, the sunset behind their shoulders. A pang of regret pinched True's heart. She'd never been to a beach.

"Mom?" A woman's voice yelled down the hall before the screen door slammed shut. Footsteps started and then stopped. "You stay upstairs," the voice commanded. Little feet hurried back to the bedroom.

True watched her mom scoot past her and turn into the hallway. "Your sister is here," June said, voice trembling.

"True?"

"Yes."

Both women were silent. The only thing True heard was the quiet hum of the diffuser and her father's wheezing. She imagined them wordlessly looking at each other, wondering what to do with the prodigal daughter. True was about to step out and intercept the pair when they rounded the corner.

Elyse examined True through dark-rimmed glasses perched high on her freckled nose. Her dark hair was pulled back and both hands were jammed into the front pockets of her scrubs. She stepped between True and their mother, glancing backwards to make sure the girls were out of sight.

"How have you been?" Clipped and formal, Elyse sounded like she was addressing a patient.

"Decent." True employed her own tactics and smiled widely. "Your daughters are beautiful, Elyse."

Her sister remained rigid but nodded once. "Thank you."

"They remind me of us."

"My girls don't run away."

True frowned. "Run away?"

"Girls," their mom chided, putting her hand on Elyse's arm.

"Do you think that I ran away?"

"Girls." The feeble but stern voice caused them both to look at their dad. "Elyse, she did not run away."

Elyse moved into the doorway of the room after June stepped next to her husband.

"You told me she ran away."

Their mom clasped hands with their dad. "We told you she *went* away."

True felt brick after brick heap onto her shoulders. Her sister didn't even know the truth—the horrible reason she was sent away, or the disgusting man who took her.

"Went away, ran away. What's the difference?" Elyse jerked her head in True's direction.

Looking up to her parents, True straightened. She swallowed the panic of telling her sister the truth in favor of cold, hard facts. "You can tell her or I will," she said, devoid of any emotion.

Elyse's face scrunched together. "What is she talking about, Mom?"

June was already crying again, her face covered by her free hand.

"I didn't tell you why she was sent away," their father said, moving the pillows behind him. "It was so long ago."

"Tell her," True prompted after he fell silent.

Elyse whipped around to face True. "You don't have the right to speak to him like that."

"I traded her," William said. "Her service for my debt."

The diffuser purred from the table, lavender trying to calm the tension in the air. True felt like she was stuck in some horrible movie, watching a terrible secret unfold—except it was her own.

Elyse's face went slack before she turned to face their parents. "What?"

Their dad looked at them, eyes watering. "There was a debt and he needed a housekeeper."

Suddenly, the room burst into noise, everyone talking over each other: Elyse demanding answers. June trying to justify the decision. William recounting his poor decisions leading up to the exchange.

True spoke once, voice strong, to cover the wavering. "You know full well what that man did to me."

Everyone stopped and looked at her.

"Sweet Moses," Elyse whispered the same thing their Mimi used to say. "I thought you ran away and left me behind." She gulped tiny breaths through her mouth.

There was no need for True to hike up her shirt and show her sister the scars underneath the delicate tattoos winding across her back. Elyse's wringing hands didn't need to feel the wrath True faced when she had tried to escape.

Her sister's face morphed from horror into fury as the pink dashed up her neck, straight to her ears. It was nearly slow motion the way she turned to their pale father.

"You traded her?"

He coughed into his sleeve. "I had debt and no way to pay it."

"How is that even legal, Dad?"

No explanation came, so Elyse laid into him with every curse imaginable, hands waving in the air to bolster her wrath.

True could only take so much hurt. "Elyse," she said, catching her sister's closest hand, then the other. She waited until they were facing one another to continue. "Hey. There's nothing that can be done now."

"The guy should be arrested, at least." Her sister's chest heaved.

A frown spread across True's lips. "He's dead."

"Well ... I suppose that's better than getting probation and being allowed to breathe air." Elyse looked over her shoulder at their dying father. "How could you do that?"

"If I could go back and let them take me instead, I would," he said flatly.

True knew he was lying. "I didn't come to fight."

"Why *are* you here?" Her mother's voice wavered.

True inhaled slowly. They'd all live if she could get them to stay with her. Holoke promised. "I live on the other side of the city and see the army outside my window every day. We've all heard the news and know what is coming."

"Maybe they'll negotiate," Elyse said, squeezing their hands together.

"They won't."

"How do you know?"

She knew Jared would deny anything she said. "I personally know the negotiations failed."

Their faces fell. Each looked up at True when they thought the others weren't looking. And they all knew that she was serious.

"I came to apologize for ..." True breathed through her nose and briefly closed her eyes. She could bring soldiers to their knees. The least she could do was tell them the truth and try to save them. "While I'm not sorry for the life I chose, I apologize for any embarrassment the rumors may have caused you."

The last words came out barely above a whisper. Nothing could take back the decision she'd made when she'd landed on the pavement after being told the loan shark had been murdered. Or the years she'd taken men into her bed to first be able to eat, and then because the money was too good to turn down.

All of True's strict work rules didn't bury her shame deep enough as her mom burst into fresh tears.

Chapter 5

As hard as True tried to work up the courage to invite the family to her home, it never fit into the conversation. June steered her daughters into the kitchen to allow their father to sleep. True was officially introduced to her nieces, who fawned over the name brand of her sweatshirt. Elyse finally pulled True to the tiny backyard to start the barbeque for lunch, after June insisted True stay.

"Well, that was awkward." Elyse cranked the gas line open and flicked the lighter towards the grill. It whooshed as the flame caught. She swore under her breath and closed the barbeque lid before looking at True. "I don't even know where to start. I can't believe Dad did that to you."

True forced a small smile. "We can't change anything now." But she'd dreamed of the *would-haves* and *could-haves* for years.

"You're a better person than I am if you can say that." Elyse tossed the lighter onto a nearby table and flopped onto a faded lawn chair.

"Certainly not better. Just . . . wanting to move forward."

"I understand that. It's what I repeated to myself when Kevin left." Elyse took a sharp breath and interrupted True's words before they started. "Don't apologize. Everyone is sorry, but it doesn't change a thing. So, I get what you're saying."

Although True disagreed and had the scars and cash to show for it, she sympathized with Elyse's stance. Instead, she took a safe route. "Tell me about your girls."

"Julianne is headstrong, exactly like you." Elyse stood as her younger daughter, Bridget, brought out hot dogs and chicken on a plate. "But this one," she said, ruffling the messy braid. "She's my little artist. Started drawing on the walls when she was two and hasn't stopped."

"Mom!" There were equal parts of embarrassment and exasperation in the eight-year-old's voice.

True hiked her eyebrows. "Don't let your mom fool you, Bridget. She used to get in trouble in school for doodling instead of taking notes."

Bridget grinned and handed over the food to her mom. "Naughty Mommy."

"You get," Elyse laughed, pushing Bridget toward the back door. She flipped open the grill lid and the heat smacked them both. With practiced motion, Elyse slid the meat onto the grates. "I can't believe you remember that."

"Did you show them where we carved out initials in the baseboard?"

Elyse sighed and closed the lid. "No. I chipped those out after you didn't come back."

True kept breathing through her nose. "Oh."

"I was so angry with you. I can't believe they lied to Ben and me."

"They technically didn't lie."

Settling back into her chair, Elyse shook her head. "You sure you're not better than me? I can't believe that you're defending them."

"What Dad did was—"

"Disgusting? Illegal? Horrible?"

"Pretty much," True said, sinking into the other chair. "But seeing the army outside my window, and knowing what's happened to the cities they've conquered ... I wanted to see you again, if only to apologize if my choice of employment had caused you any embarrassment."

Elyse scoffed. "You didn't have much of a choice."

"I could've gone to school. Become a nurse." True nodded toward Elyse's scrubs. "I took the easiest path to money."

"But you didn't get into drugs?"

"No." True hesitated. "I'd seen too much of the aftermath when I was young."

"You talk so formally," Elyse laughed.

"I tried to rise above my job. I wanted a certain level of respect and so I had to act and live in a way that attracted that type of clientele."

"Wow." Elyse's eyebrows nearly met her hairline. "Clientele. That sounds weird."

"It is what it is."

"Celebrities?"

"Some."

"Anyone I've heard of?"

"Certainly."

Elyse leaned forward. "Going to tell me who?"

True reflected her sister's position. "Never." A genuine smile eased across her face when Elyse laughed. This is why she'd come. She needed them to survive. "Can I ask you a favor?"

Her sister stood to attend the barbeque. "Depends on the favor."

With Elyse's back turned, True hoped her invitation would flow easier. "I'd like you to come visit me. My house is fortified with rebar drilled into the bedrock."

"That's a random fact."

"It means my walls won't fall down the cliff."

"Still totally random."

"Well," True said, stretching. "You can see the entire valley from the windows."

Elyse turned, spatula in hand. "Can you really see the army?"

True nodded, looking at the flames licking up to burn the meat. "It is massive." She thought of Holoke standing in front of her before he disappeared down the ladder.

"We can come tomorrow. What time?"

"Whatever fits into your schedule."

June popped her head out of the door. "Is it ready yet?"

"Yup, just get me a clean plate."

Back inside, the ladies sat on the same vinyl chairs they'd occupied years before. Elyse filled in True on the family details, none the wiser that her elder sister simply nodded out of politeness. Their mom fussed in the kitchen, wiping the clean counters and checking on her husband. True asked questions to make Elyse talk while she watched her sister's hands wave around during the conversation. William made a short appearance on his way to the bathroom, bobbing his head when he met True's gaze.

"Here!" A few hours later, Bridget slid a drawing of a unicorn across the table.

True placed both hands on the paper and traced the words at the bottom of the page: Aunt True. She'd never been an actual aunt before and Bridget's drawing plucked at brand new guilt. "I don't even know your birthday," she whispered, looking through her tears to the bewildered girl with freckles.

"October twentieth." Bridget pecked True's cheek with her bow-shaped lips and tore down the hallway and up the stairs, shrieking at Julianne.

When True's phone vibrated in her sweatshirt pocket, she jerked. "Excuse me," she said, stepping away to seek refuge in the bathroom. Jared sent a brief text that they'd found the spies' trail and would capture them soon. She knew he was lying to impress her—he would've sent a picture if they were actually prisoners.

True pocketed her phone and ran the water from the tap. She rinsed her face with both hands. After using the towel on the hook, she looked at the mirror for a moment. An errant drop of water fell from her nose. She could book them all on a bus out of the city tonight or tomorrow. It'd be easier to get them to go see Ben. All she had to do was talk them into it.

The news blared from the small radio in the kitchen when True returned. June rinsed the sink and dried it as the man announced the President's declaration to restrict people from leaving the city.

"It is for the safety of our citizens, in case those leaving are actually spies for the enemy," the broadcaster said.

"Mom, True wants us to come over tomorrow," Elyse said, pushing the leftovers into the fridge.

June looked up, eyes wide.

"I'd like you to see the view from my place." True employed her soothing tone and slight shift of shoulders. "I'll make dinner or lunch. Or even breakfast if you want to come over early."

Elyse looked back and forth, like she was watching a tennis match. Her mom remained silent.

"For heaven's sake, Mom. It's not like she's gonna kill us." Elyse yawned wide and stretched her shoulders. "I'll be there for lunch with the girls around noon."

True rattled off her phone number. Having Elyse and the girls was better than no one. Ben would be safe until the army advanced since he lived a couple of hours away.

By the time Elyse walked True out to the cab she'd called for, twilight wrapped the sky in a blaze of pink and orange. The heat radiated from the sidewalk as the sisters hugged again. True had lost count of how many times Elyse touched her arm or they embraced. Their mom had silently flitted around the perimeter of her daughters.

"Tomorrow at noon."

"I'll try and make something the girls will like."

"They like anything that has the word nuggets or cheese."

True let her laughter hide her dread at leaving. They might change their minds after she left. Or she could wake up from this perfect dream.

Elyse hiccupped a sob. "I don't want to let you go."

Inhaling the familiar scent of her sister's old shampoo in the ponytail, True eased back and held Elyse's face in her hands. "Never again. I will always protect you."

"You and your reinforced house?" Elyse swiped at her tears.

"Wait until I show you my fire escape." True smiled her bravest smile and winked. The cabbie beeped his horn. "I'll see you tomorrow."

"Probably every day from now on."

"That's fine. But lunch first." True opened the car door.

"All right. Hey, True?"

She turned to look at her sister again. "Yes?"

"I'm sorry I stopped loving you. I never should have stopped."

True grabbed her sister's hand. She could barely speak past the lump in her throat. "I will see you tomorrow."

"Text me when you get home."

"Okay, *Mom*," True laughed, ducking into the cab.

The ride back was quick and True headed straight to the shower. She wept into the tiled walls. Holoke's promise, her father's apology, Elyse's visit—it was nothing she ever thought would happen in less than forty-eight hours. If it weren't for the impending demolition of the city, it might be a dream come true.

Stars twinkled overhead by the time True dressed and went to the rooftop to eat her dinner. The metal flaps waved along to the singing tree's song. Far across the valley, the army remained exactly where they had been the day before. She wondered where Holoke and Conley were hunkered down. The same weird feeling that had allowed her to open the door blanketed her fears: they were fine and she would be saved from the destruction.

"At least you have a giant nightlight to guide you back to the camp," she said aloud, toasting her wine glass to camp's beacon shining in the night.

Foregoing certain the misery of the news recap, True turned on some soft music in her loft. She picked up the book on Queen Sheba from her nightstand. When she sank into the armchair, she turned her nose into the padded back to catch a trace of Holoke.

The next morning, True checked her phone. Elyse had sent pictures of the girls tucked into the same bed, arms and legs tangled. A lazy grin spread across True's face. She much rather preferred these photos to the ones her clientele sent.

The chicken nuggets were in the oven and the mac and cheese was on low when Elyse knocked and waved into the monitor. The girls shoved past their mom.

"Aunt True, your house is so fancy!"

"Where's the bathroom? Are the faucets made of gold?"

"Your television is behind a curtain? That's so cool!"

"Why is there a bed in the corner?"

True stopped at the kitchen counter. "It's called a lounging couch, or a daybed. This one is Balinese." It wasn't a flat out lie. The bed *had* been a daybed when she'd originally purchased it. "It's made of teakwood."

Julianne squinted at the bed. "There are a lot of pillows."

"Look it up. They are usually like a bed, with lots of pillows." True had dug out the extra ones from the workshop before falling asleep the night before.

"I would, but Mom won't let me have a phone yet."

"Me neither," Bridget said. She'd climbed on the bed and commenced bouncing.

"You girls hungry? We can eat and then I'll show you around."

Lunch was a frantic affair. The girls inhaled their food, barely chewing between bites.

Elyse wandered to the window. She set her glass on the sill. "There's so many of them."

True looked up from cutting a pan of brownies.

"It doesn't look this bad on the news," Elyse said.

"Girls? Want to go up those stairs to my bedroom? I have a few books up there."

The pair scrambled from the barstools and clamored up the stairs. Overhead, their feet rushed back and forth. She heard the familiar rattling of the heavy workshop door handle.

True joined her sister at the window downstairs. Elyse worked her way through the glass of wine and sighed, eyes glued to the foreigners. "They are coming for us, aren't they?"

They looked at each other. True didn't want to lie. "No doubt."

"Will we survive?"

"I have no idea." It all depended on the promise of a complete stranger.

Elyse smiled. "Is that why you told me about the reinforced walls?"

True laughed and pinched her nose. Silence was her price. "It's the best shot we have, since the President won't let anyone out."

"Mom! Julianne won't let me sit in the chair!"

The women climbed the stairs and solved the fight by sending each girl across the loft.

"Looks like the bedspread we used to have," Elyse said, fingering the shabby calico.

"That was the plan."

"What's in here?" Bridget jiggled the workshop door handle again.

"Bridget, stop," Elyse said.

"No, it's okay. It's my workshop, but there's metal everywhere. You might get cut, so we'll have to go in another day, after I've cleaned it up."

Elyse cocked her head. "Metal?"

"Yeah. I've learned to sculpt with it."

Bridget's attention span waned and she went to the window. Julianne curled into herself with a book in the armchair.

"Huh." Elyse leaned onto the workshop door.

"Well, it's not like my line of work has a retirement plan." True smiled at the girls, who were lost in their own worlds. "Besides, I was saving to move somewhere else and start over."

"Where?"

"I hadn't decided. Depended on the currency exchange and real estate."

Elyse shook her head. "I can't believe we are talking about this."

"Well, it's better to talk about the future than about what's outside the window."

"Agreed." Elyse's phone tweedled from her pocket. She showed True the screen. It was Ben. "Hi! Yeah, I'm at True's now."

True left the trio upstairs and took the empty wine glasses down to the sink. She washed the dishes while Bridget's feet ran from one side of the loft to the other and back again. It was so strange to have noise in a house built for one.

"Sorry about that," Elyse said, coming down the stairs. "He wants to come, but can't get through."

"That's probably for the better." True put the dishes in the soapy water to soak. Ben and his family were safe for now. One less family to have to get into her house when everything was set in motion.

The sisters spent so long catching up that the girls reminded them about dinner. True made them smiley face pancakes. While the girls gobbled down their meal, True joined Elyse at the window once more. A tear tracked down Elyse's face when she looked from the army to her children. True held her sister's hand and tossed a silent prayer to Holoke's God that everything would work out.

Chapter 6

The girls squealed with delight when True served them pastries the next morning.

"Thanks for watching them," Elyse said, motioning for the cab to stay at the curb. "My lunch is at noon and I'm off at five-thirty." She looked around the room and True knew she was checking for clients.

"No one here but us girls. We'll be hanging out here, doing our nails and hair and other girlie stuff."

"Real nice. Mani-pedi day and I'm going to be stuck looking at mysterious diaper rashes and swabbing for cultures." Elyse craned her head to look at her daughters, swinging their legs from the barstools at the kitchen counter. "Have fun and be good!"

The pair didn't even glance up as they gobbled through the buttery layers.

Elyse shrugged and offered a haphazard wave as she ducked into the cab. True watched the car until it turned down the street. This time of day was foreign to her. She wasn't used to the waking hours, the hustle of people getting to work. Usually, she'd be fast asleep behind the thick, soundproof brick walls of her home.

"Aunt True, Julianne is taking my breakfast."

True shut the door and threw the bolt. "You don't have to steal hers," she said, grabbing the older girl's plate. "There are more." Proof followed her words as she slid another pastry onto the plate.

Julianne mumbled her gratitude through a stuffed mouth. True was certain it was more manners than appreciation, as she watched Julianne's eyes dart around the lower level of her home. True made a cup of black coffee and watched the older sister inventory the floor. She smiled into the rim of the mug, silently applauding her niece's distrust.

"Well, you're here for the day. What would you like to do first?" True polished off her coffee and lowered the cup to the sink.

Bridget wiped the crumbs from her mouth with the back of her hand. "I've never had a mani-pedi."

Julianne scoffed. "You don't even know what one is."

"Do too! It's when you get your fingernails and toenails painted." Her little scowl nearly made True smile. "You've never had one either. You don't even like nail polish."

"Oh, I am sorry if you don't want to do that," True said.

"It's fine." Julianne mowed through the last bite of her third pastry.

"You can read if you don't want me to paint your nails." True cleared their plates and hid her grin. It was like looking at herself more than a decade ago, all moody and wanting to vault into the teenager years.

Without a word, Julianne slid off her stool and slinked up the stairs. Bridget happily chattered alongside True while the dishes were washed and dried. The pair picked polish colors from the bathroom and settled in near the window.

Somewhere between flailing her tiny hands to dry and picking out a vivid purple for her toes, Bridget looked out of the window. "Hey, Aunt True?"

There'd been about nine-million questions before this one. "Yes, peanut?"

"Those guys out there are moving."

True shook the polish bottle and stood. She shuffled from her spot to see where Bridget pointed. It took every ounce of control to keep the tiny bottle from dropping when she saw the dust cloud behind the army, as it advanced towards the city.

Her phone chirped. The polish dropped and broke. Purple splattered across her wall, bare feet, and jeans. A government emergency broadcast message lit up her phone as she pulled it from her pocket. She didn't hear what Bridget was saying as she read the text:

SHELTER IN PLACE. MORE INFORMATION WILL FOLLOW.

"Aunt True." Bridget pulled on True's hand. "Aunt True!"

True glanced to the innocent face. "I'm sorry. What did you say?"

"Your jeans are ruined."

Looking back out of the window, True thought more than her clothes were destroyed. "It's okay. I'll go change after I clean this up."

The nail polish remover singed her nose as she wiped the purple globs. Her hands were stained the same color. "Hold tight. I have to go wash my hands and change pants."

"Okay. I'm gonna stay here and watch those tank thingies."

The text scrolled across her phone again on the counter as she dunked her hands under the water in the bathroom sink. Holoke wouldn't reneg on his promise. He couldn't. She'd hidden them.

The ringing phone made True jerk her elbow into the wall.

"You guys okay?" Elyse was out of breath. In the background, it sounded like she was in an overcrowded marketplace, not a doctor's office. People were yelling, children bawling.

"Yeah, yeah. We're perfectly fine."

"Do you know why they sent that broadcast?"

True pulled in a breath and held it. They only needed to be in her house and they would be safe. "I do. But you need to be somewhere quiet for us to talk. Can you do that right now?"

Elyse swore at someone nearby. True heard a click, followed by Elyse's heavy sigh. "Made it to my office. Spill it."

"The army is advancing toward the city."

Her sister's language rivaled a seasoned soldier. "I'll be there as soon as I can."

"We are really all right. The girls are fine. I was just getting ready to paint Bridget's toes when she saw them."

"Is Julianne okay?"

"I'm washing up in the bathroom. I dropped polish all over myself when I saw. I'll go check on her now." True waved to Bridget on her way up the staircase. Julianne was sideways across the armchair, one leg on the floor and the other draped over the armrest. "How's it going up here?" True asked.

Julianne didn't even lower her book. "Fine."

"Your mom is on the phone and asked."

"I'm fine."

"Okay. Let me know if you need anything."

The silence escorted True downstairs. She switched on her monitors and watched the panic in the streets. "It's crazy out there."

"I'm packing up my stuff," Elyse said.

"I hope they let you through. Come as soon you can. I'll even call in favors if you need them. We are safe and have lots of food."

"Gotta go. Ben is calling me. He must've heard it from someone."

"Call me."

"I will."

True held the phone to her ear for a few moments after her sister hung up. Without a doubt, the city was in chaos from such a random message. She turned off the monitors.

Bridget hummed and bounced from one foot to the other. "I can't even count how many there are!" Her voice was full of wonder before she spun around. "Can I go pick another color for my toes?"

"Of course." True moved to the spot Bridget had stood. There were tiny patches of warmth on the tiles and the smell of remover still permeated the air. All she could think about was Holoke's promise to allow her to live as the dust cloud lifted higher and higher behind the endless convoy of vehicles.

"What's out there?"

True looked over her shoulder to Julianne, who was halfway down the stairs. The little investigator would probably be able to detect a lie. "The army is advancing."

Julianne's brown eyes widened and she pressed herself into the wall. "Toward the city?"

"Yes."

"They're going to kill us all." Her young voice slipped up an octave.

"We don't know that—"

"They kill everyone. I've seen the news and we were told that in school."

True fully turned and faced Julianne. "You don't know that. They could negotiate surrender this time. We are a large city."

"Who's a large city?" Bridget emerged, clutching a blue bottle.

"Shut up," Julianne snapped.

"That was unnecessary." True folded her arms across her chest. Suddenly, she knew that she looked like her mother, minus the red apron.

The phone in True's pocket buzzed. Jared sent her a short text. He was back in the city and would be by later. She contemplated her answer as Julianne crossed the floor and grabbed the sill until her knuckles turned white. True responded that she wouldn't be available. When it vibrated once and then twice, she knew it would be him calling, so she went into the bathroom again.

"What do you mean you won't be available?" She could imagine the shade of pink his cheeks were turning as he spat into the mouthpiece.

"I do make other plans, Jared."

"Not when it comes to me."

"I apologize, but I have a previous engagement."

"Cancel it."

"I will not."

"True." He sounded like a wild tomcat in the alley, growling a warning as another cat approached.

"It is impossible."

"Oh, you'll make time for me."

The phone disconnected.

True stared at the mirror, knowing his temper had been stoked. She'd seen the bruised soldiers under his command, the ones who remained silent and unmoving when she'd mentioned General Kohl. He'd never raised a hand to her, but the rage simmered beneath his feral smiles and generous cash.

He was coming. She was sure of it.

"Hey, girls, want to see my workshop?" True motioned upstairs. Bridget forgot about her toenails and tore up the stairs. True waited for Julianne to mope her way and shepherded her to the loft. Keying in the access code, True told the girls to watch for sharp metal pieces. Jared would be pounding on the door any second.

"Julianne." True dropped her voice. She waited for her niece to turn around. "I don't want to frighten Bridget or you, but I need you both to stay in here for a while. Someone is going to be at my door in a few minutes and I need you both to stay in here and be quiet."

The smaller pair of eyes rounded, but Julianne remained silent. She took a long breath in through her nose and bobbed her chin once.

"Thank you. Here is my phone. Don't answer any texts. Only use it if I'm not back in ten minutes. Don't call your mom yet. I promise that I will call her, and you can listen if you'd like." True's words rushed out. "I need you to do that."

"Yeah." Julianne nearly whispered her answer. "Are you going to be okay?"

True threw a smile across her lips. "Of course I will be. He's just a grumpy man who might yell. But, I'm the only one with the door code."

"Okay. I'll keep Bridget busy."

"Don't touch that thing. It's old and persnickety." She pointed to the green paint-chipped MIG welder in the corner. "I need to take care of something really quick, then I'll take you to the roof," True said as Bridget spun an old windmill on the wall.

The steel door downstairs rang out as a metal baton beat into it. True nodded to Julianne and hauled the door closed. She breathed through her nose as she descended, the tempo of Jared's bashing increasing in tempo.

True turned on the monitors. She could hear his muffled yelling through the door. People on the street stopped to stare. Pushing the intercom button, his grunts echoed into the room.

"Calm down. I was using the restroom."

He swiveled his face to the nearest camera. "Open this door."

"Will you be civil?"

Jared pulled his jacket straight. "We need to speak."

True could barely keep her hands from shaking as she slid the bolt back. The door handle turned and Jared shoved past her as she teetered backwards.

"What do you mean, you're unavailable?" He was in dirty khakis and his graying hair was uncombed. "Why is the bed over there?"

She clasped her hands in front of her. "I simply have other plans that I cannot cancel."

"Who?"

"My business is not yours."

"If it interferes with mine, it is." He glanced at the buttons on her shirt.

"No, General Kohl, it isn't."

His face flushed even more deeply and he stepped within a breath of her face. "You whore. I will ruin you." He smelled like liquor and stale air. When his shoulder twitched, True braced for impact.

"If we survive this, I doubt anything you do will have an effect on my life." True fought to keep her tone even and pleasant.

Jared snorted and stomped back out of the still open door.

True pushed the door closed and sent the bolt home. She paused and rested her head on the cool steel, then climbed the stairs. When the beeping buttons released the latch, the girls looked at her from their spot on the floor. They were surrounded by her first efforts with the singing tree tubes.

"Would you like to see the sculpture I made from those?" True nodded to the metal parts.

Julianne pressed the phone into True's hand as she stood. The faintest collection of tears crowded the corner of the girl's eyes.

"Yes!" Bridget popped up like an exploding kernel.

The girls waited for True to unlatch the roof access. They all squinted into the bright sunlight as they emerged. The breeze sang into the tubes of the tree.

"Did you make that?" Bridget skittered over to the twisting sculpture. "It sounds so pretty."

"The sounds are all different, depending on the way the wind blows, how fast it is blowing, and which tube the wind hits. See how they are all different lengths?" True walked them around the tree. "The trunk is hollow inside. I didn't want to make it so heavy that it crashed through my roof."

"I could hide inside?" Bridget was already climbing before True answered.

Julianne watched the scales on the box where Conley hid. "Why do some of them look like dragon scales?"

"Oh the coloring? That is because of the heat from the welder and I was experimenting." True shielded her eyes.

"I like it. It's like it's dancing."

"Then I'll call it 'Julianne's Dancing Box.'"

Julianne looked up and smiled, a tiny dimple burrowing deep in her cheek.

"What's that?" Bridget pointed out to the valley.

True looked past the little finger, moving toward the wall. She didn't even bother to try and count the tanks or trucks that had stopped within a mile of the city. The camp spread as far to the right as to the left. It was a well-oiled machine, laid in a well-organized pattern. Tents were erected with efficiency that'd make Jared glare in jealousy.

She knew Holoke was down there somewhere. Shading her eyes, she regretted not owning a pair of binoculars. Maybe he'd already checked to see if the ladder was still hanging from the fire escape. The metal rungs clapped against the bricks below her perch. She double-checked her messages.

"They stopped." Julianne bumped into True's elbow.

Bridget knocked into the other one. "Why?"

"I have no idea," True said.

"Do you hear that?" Bridget gripped the top of the wall, her face almost able to clear the side. "What's that sound?"

It was low and vibrating, like an endless bow pulled across a standing bass string. True watched as a thin, dark cloud rose from the army. The closer the cloud came to the base of the cliffs, the louder and higher the pitch.

The emergency alert tone from her phone made the trio jerk. True held it for them all to read:

STAY INSIDE. SHELTER IN PLACE. MORE INFORMATION TO FOLLOW.

By the time she looked back up, True knew that it was no cloud. A massive formation of quad-copter drones soared upwards toward her home.

Julianne stepped backwards, grabbing Bridget. "We gotta go inside," she said, her voice wavering.

True stood, transfixed. "I'll be down in a minute." She peered as the drones rose above the tallest buildings. Little cameras swiveled from their bellies. All of the sudden, the air erupted with an old-fashioned, instrumental battle song from the hovering craft. True slapped her hands over her ears. It sounded oddly patriotic.

In a coordination as precise as the army that guided them, the drones moved from her home to the north, along the edge of the city. The whine of the engines and their songs faded as they circled, at times disappearing behind the looming clock tower at the college and then the sleek skyscraper that housed the President. Her stomach lurched its contents and True concentrated to keep from vomiting as the pack completed its perimeter of the city. The drones hovered, the music stopped, then they returned to their base.

"Why'd they do that?" True hadn't even noticed Julianne at her side again until the girl slid her hand into True's.

"Probably inspecting the city," True said, squeezing their hands together.

"Can we go inside? Bridget is crying. She's scared."

True nodded, unable to admit that she was too.

Chapter 7

Elyse arrived before dinner, duffel bags in hand. "I'm thinking your random, reinforced walls are a good choice," she said, crushing True into a hug. "But I'm not sure Mom and Dad will come."

"How's Ben?"

"He's mad he can't get us out."

"At least he's safe there."

The girls tumbled down the stairs once they heard their mother and latched onto Elyse's waist.

"Hello, my lovelies. How was your day with your Aunt True?" She pressed a kiss into their heads and True smiled to push back the whisper of longing for a child of her own.

Bridget scrambled across the room and vaulted onto the lounging couch. "This is the best spot in the whole place. She even let us eat here."

"You know you're only supposed to eat in the kitchen."

True cocked her head. "My house, my rules. They can eat wherever they want, as long as they clean up."

"Great. Play the nice aunt card." Elyse moved the bags next to Bridget's roost while Julianne climbed next to her sister. They both resumed reading the books they'd found earlier.

True leaned against the wall. "I have fourteen years of catching up. I'll use whatever is within my means. Besides, I remember sneaking up food while we read. Mom would always go on and on about ants, but we never had them."

Elyse sighed. "Speaking of Mom, when I was packing, Dad was being a ... pickle licker." She glanced at her daughters, who giggled into their books. "It's rude to listen in."

"You're right in front of us," Julianne said, without lifting her eyes from the pages.

The elder pair of sisters moved to the window. Elyse swore under her breath at the sight. "I can't believe this is happening, that the President didn't stop this."

"I'm not sure he could've prevented it."

"Did you see the drones?"

"Yes."

"How many were there? I haven't had time to check the news."

True kept her eyes on the army. "More than I could count. Over one hundred, easily."

Elyse glanced over to her daughters and dropped her voice. "Dad said he wouldn't come. Said that if he was going to die, it'd be at home like he'd planned on doing."

"Stubborn to the end."

"And yet, you somehow don't hate him."

Turning to her sister, True looked over Elyse's shoulder at the girls. "There are things that don't matter anymore to me. One is hate. Don't think that I have forgotten what he did. Or that you and Ben had vacations and graduations and weddings that I didn't get to have. But what's the sense in it now?"

The sunset washed Elyse's face in soft orange colors. Her hands still smelled like disinfectant soap from the hospital. They simply stared at each other's faces, eyes darting back and forth from one eyeball to the other, like they'd done so many years before. Elyse finally grinned. "Okay. I can hate him for you, but I still wish they'd come. Even if he slept on the floor. I think if there's any chance of riding this out, these will hold up." She slapped a hand to the bricks.

"Momma, you should see Aunt True's singing tree. It's the coolest thing ever." Bridget wedged her slim body between them.

Elyse's eyebrow shot up. "Coolest thing ever? I should probably see it then."

True led the troop back to the roof, Bridget the perpetual tour guide. "That's her old welder and it is touchy, but it makes dragon scales."

"A singing tree and dragon scales. My, my, sister, you've been busy."

"It's only on my down time." True grunted as she shoved the hatch open.

Right on cue, the tubes caught a breeze and filled the twilight with a somber melody.

"That is amazing," Elyse said, walking around it.

The noises from the encampment below climbed the cliffs, murmuring under the varying tones. True went to the wall and looked down while the girls showed Elyse how Julianne's box opened up and the hollow tree trunk. The army's spotlight flickered to life, shooting a beam straight into the open sky.

For the millionth time, it seemed, True checked to make sure the rope dangled from the fire escape. She almost imagined a burst of flashlight from far below.

"What'cha looking at?" Elyse sidled up, their bodies touching shoulder to calf.

True wanted to live. She wanted to see Elyse's girls grow up and get married. She wanted a husband. Instead, she replied, "There are so many of them."

"Wonder why they waited so long to advance."

"Gathering intelligence."

"You say that like you know something."

True paused before she answered, turning over the response she longed to tell her sister. "It's my business to know soldiers, so I've picked up a few things along the years."

"I envy you in a way," Elyse said. Both women stared at the enemy below. "I don't know everything that happened. Maybe you'll tell me, maybe you won't. But I never left Mom and Dad's. Pregnant at fifteen and nineteen, divorced, and living in our brother's bedroom after he moved out. I have a lousy nursing certificate that barely pays for our insurance. You have all of this."

"You have your girls." True reached over and clasped her sister's hand. "And that is more than I will ever have."

Elyse stilled. Then, she squeezed True's hand.

Their phones simultaneously shrilled out another emergency alert:

SHELTER IN PLACE. BROADCAST IN 30 MINUTES WITH FURTHER INFO.

"Let's get the girls fed before this announcement," True suggested.

After a hurried dinner, True ran a bath with bubbles for Bridget. Upon learning she and her sister would be sharing the lounging couch to sleep on, Julianne retreated upstairs to brood. "She kicks like a blind ninja," the pre-teen said, stomping to emphasize each syllable.

"Does she ever remind you of me?" True washed a dish and handed it to Elyse.

"Most days. Especially when she finds the meaning to fancy words and uses them to piss me off."

They turned their attention to the cell phone propped on the counter. The President's well-lit face filled the screen. He recounted the week's events. "There are 40,000 troops equipped for battle right outside of the city's boundaries. I cannot, with a clear conscience, allow my citizens to be put into further danger."

The camera switched to images of the drones, then the one and only main road leaving the city. Burning cars and twisted metal hulks blocked the route. "We are not entirely sure that there are not spies working within our walls. With that said, there will officially be no exits allowed. Nor will anyone be granted entry."

"He'll let us all die because of his pride." Elyse slapped a clean fork onto the counter.

Soldiers stood at attention near the city entrance. Once more, the President sat at his desk, hands folded and a flag on his lapel. "Stand fast, my friends. We will conquer this foe. Good night."

Elyse's vulgar thoughts toward the President's speech were interrupted by a soft knock at the front door. True flicked on the monitors and immediately opened the door.

"Mom?"

Her mother pulled a small suitcase on wheels and a huge purse weighting down the opposite shoulder. Sweat dotted her forehead. Behind her, True watched as her dad crawled out of a taxi.

Elyse yanked the door wider. "And hell freezes over."

True ignored the remark and took the suitcase, leading the way in. "I'm glad you came."

"We want to be together," their mother said. She waited for her husband at the door.

He latched onto her elbow. Sweat glistened his upper lip and he wheezed with every step.

"Over here." True swept her arm toward the lounging couch and straightened the pillows the girls had mashed.

He wilted onto the mattress and his eyelids closed. "Just give me a minute to catch my breath."

As the cab drove away, True closed and bolted the door. She'd done it. They were all here and everything would work out.

⌣

The noise was nearly unbearable the first night. After trying every possible position, earplugs, and a pillow over her head, True prowled her loft. The girls slept in her bed, Bridget with her head at the foot of the bed and Julianne triumphantly "where the head should be." Elyse and True robbed the pillows from the bed-couch downstairs and covered them with blankets. The lumpy substitute was nothing close to the memory foam her nieces nestled into next to the princess nightlight Elyse had brought along for Bridget.

Early the next morning, her father's coughing woke the rest of the family. Everything was loud—breakfast, figuring a showering schedule. Even the forced conversations the adults had ended up with raised voices. Elyse took the offense, no matter the topic, and turned it against her parent's decision for True. Several times, she stormed off for a walk, since the hospital clinic was closed.

On the second morning with the family, Ben joined in the argument via speakerphone against their father for his reprehensible decision, even though True begged her siblings to stop.

By the third day, the girls were bored. The army flew their drones around the city every day, music blaring. The little ones wanted to see their friends. Elyse wanted to work. True wanted solitude or a moment of quiet. Her cell phone sat idle in her pocket, eerily silent without Jared's texts.

Day four, True excused herself for an afternoon trip to Mr. Aoki's before the drone army advanced. The air was stagnant, as if it were weighed down with boredom. No cars moved around, but small groups of people gathered near front doorways. True tucked her chin down as she walked and listened. They complained about the President and the army. Mothers were stuck at home with kids. Kids were stuck at home with nothing to do. And life had come to a wretched standstill.

Mr. Aoki offered her what he could from his nearly bare shelves. "You are one of my best customers, so I'll take you into the back room." True picked through his meager selection and overpaid him.

On the walk back, the music preceded the drones, echoing down the roadways. Children and adults immigrated onto the sidewalks, rocks in hand. In small droves, they ran behind the quad-copters, pitching stones into the air. They yelled obscenities as the drones moved away, rocks never hitting their intended targets.

True hurried and passed a lone cab on the street. She let herself into her home and saw the rumpled, empty lounging couch. Elyse sat at the kitchen counter, eating cereal and reading the box.

"Where are they?"

"Dad said he wanted to go home."

The lights flickered in the house. Elyse's spoon hung in midair as she looked up to the ceiling. True hesitated when the power wavered a second time.

"It's okay," she whispered, placing her bag near the kitchen sink. Had the army infiltrated their power substation? Jared said there were backup generators as fail-safes.

The army's battle hymn, as June called it, grew louder as the drones completed their circuit. It stopped altogether before their engines slid down the cliffs and back to their basecamp.

Elyse resumed eating. "I wonder if they pick dinner time for dramatic effect."

True called their mom's cell phone and it went straight to voicemail. She tried the house and the answering machine picked up.

"Come on."

"You won't change their minds."

"I can try."

"You give them more effort than they gave you."

"Why can't you let it go?" True turned and faced her sister. "I was the one they basically sold off. I've fought my own battles for years, and this one was over long before now."

"You want us to leave too?" Elyse's stool tipped over and clattered against the tile.

"No! Please don't go." The groceries thumped into the sink in her haste to get around the counter. "Please don't go," she repeated, barely keeping her voice from breaking.

"Fine. But since they're gone, we're not sleeping on the floor anymore. My back is killing me." Elyse's smile tipped up one side of her lips.

That night, the girls refused to sleep alone in the loft, so the adult sisters shoved and prodded the massive mattress up the stairs, plopping it on the floor, next to the bed. After a second shower, they collapsed next to each other in the near dark.

True stared at the ceiling. She'd never noticed the tiny cracks that raced away from the light fixture. And she would never get to hang the chandelier sitting in the corner of the workshop, waiting to be rewired.

Elyse rolled over, her breath on True's shoulder. "You awake?" Her whisper cut through the girls' breathing on the bed nearby.

"Yeah."

"Do you think that we'll survive?"

The cell phone was warm in True's hand. She prayed silently to Holoke's God-with-a-big-G that he wouldn't forget their promise. "I hope so. I really wanted to start my life over."

Scooching closer, Elyse's chin nearly touched True. "Really?"

"Yeah. I have money saved up. I was going to move, far away. Maybe across the world, where no one knew me." She rolled to face her sister. True laid her hand on Elyse's cheek. "That was before I got my family back."

"I don't want my girls to die," Elyse said. Her eyes flicked up to the bed. "It's not fair. They have everything in front of them." Her voice cracked and her nostrils flared before a tear pushed out.

"I wish I could tell you why, but I think we will come out okay."

"Are you a psychic now?"

"Just a gut feeling."

Elyse sniffed hard. "Maybe it's hunger. You forgot to eat." Her laughter jiggled the bed. "You going to go look at the fire escape again? You always do that when we talk about the army."

"I do?"

"Yeah. It was weird at first. But then I thought you're making sure we can escape. And I'm good with that."

True sighed. "Me too. We need to figure out how to distract the army so we can scale a cliff. Then live in the woods without food or tools."

"Sounds easy enough. I've seen a few TV shows. I can probably make fire."

"Fire is good."

Elyse's breathing grew slow and steady before her soft snores started. True inched out of the bed and to the second story window and checked the ladder again.

Chapter 8

True's headache pulsed behind her closed eyes. She was tired of pacing every night. When her phone vibrated on her pillow, a week after the drones first appeared, she had to persuade her eyes to open.

GET READY

She shifted onto her elbow to look at the screen again. It was the number she wasn't allowed to answer.

The smooth wood floor chilled her feet as she snuck to the window and peeked through the curtains. The army camp was shrinking as tents disappeared to the ground. Tiny soldiers ran back and forth between trucks. True's lungs felt heavy as she let the curtain fall back.

Tiptoeing back to the mattress, True rubbed Elyse's arm until she stirred. She placed her finger across her sister's lips. They crept downstairs, Elyse trailing True to the window.

"They are packing up," True whispered.

"They are going away?"

"I don't think so."

"What?"

"I think ... I think they will be attacking the city today."

Elyse mumbled a pretty line of curses, scrubbing her eyes with both hands.

"Can you get Mom and Dad to come back?" True erased the message in case anyone found her phone.

"No. I tried again last night. Dad won't budge."

True swallowed. It wasn't supposed to be like this. Everyone in her house would be safe. She cranked open the window and pressed her nose into the screen. The distant hum of engines rose. "We should pack."

"I have the duffel bags."

"No, lighter. I don't know how we will travel. Or how long." True picked through her words with caution, unwilling to jeopardize her side of the bargain. Their God would surely hear.

They dumped the contents of the girls' small backpacks and rolled clothes into them.

"No," Elyse said, surveying their work. "We should do half food and mostly underwear and socks. I've seen too many zombie shows."

True smiled and obeyed. It was happening and it felt like the last six days hadn't even passed. There was a comfortable routine with the four females in her house and she didn't want it to end.

When the girls finally tumbled down the stairs, True headed up. She threw open the curtains while stuffing clothes into an oversized shopping bag with chickens on the front. She tied on a pair of sneakers and headed to the roof for a better view.

The humming was so low at first that True didn't realize the annoying sound until it was much closer. Tiny red and green lights blinked, distinguishing the camouflaged drones from the background of the valley. She moved away from the singing sculpture to the half wall of her roof. There were too many to count—the small quad-propellered ones leading several bulkier drones with something more sinister strapped to their undersides. She knew those sleek cylinders from the one Jared had casually tossed across the bed one evening.

"This'll level the entire block."

"And yet, you toss it onto my bed."

"It needs an impact to detonate and I doubt your memory foam is hiding something."

His conversation bounced around in True's mind as the wave of drones buzzed overhead and into the familiar circle around the perimeter of the city. She wondered if anyone else saw those bombs. Did their hands shake as much as hers?

After they moved away, True looked down to the army. The far left flank inched toward the main road into the city. Black-clad soldiers fell into rowed formations. Clanking tank skids echoed up the cliffs. Belches of diesel smoke from their trucks puffed away on the wind. Each vehicle filed into a single mechanical caterpillar, the men its shuffling legs, crawling to consume its enemy.

The phone in her pocket erupted with continuous emergency alerts. In the street below her house, True glanced over the opposite wall as the citizens on the stoops fled indoors, screaming for their children. She tried dialing her mom, but all circuits were busy.

"True!" Elyse popped up from the hatch. "I can't get through to Mom and Dad."

TRUE

"Me neither."

"I have the backpacks ready."

"They are armed this time."

Elyse's jaw went slack. "What?"

"There are more drones, different ones. They have ... bombs."

"How do you know that?"

"I've had an officer show me a prototype."

"You could be wrong."

"Elyse." True grabbed her sister by both shoulders. "We need to get downstairs. Figure out where we are going to hide and block the windows." It felt like someone else was using her monotonous voice, demanding compliance.

They both checked their phones on the way down. The most recent emergency messages from the government were from just before the drone army arrival. Neither could get a signal. Downstairs, the girls finished their cereal and bickered about who had to wash the bowls.

"Go get dressed." Elyse's voice was low and clipped.

Julianne hesitated. Bridget flew up the stairs.

"I don't have time for this, Jules. Things are about to happen. Bad things. I need you to get dressed in pants and tennis shoes. Tie a sweatshirt around your waist. And get your sister dressed."

The small brown eyes widened.

"Sweetie," True said, stepping towards her. "We don't have much time. Go get dressed and wait on the bed."

"What's going on?" Tears pricked the corners of Julianne's eyes.

"Go," Elyse ordered.

Julianne disappeared after Bridget. Elyse yanked out anything easy to eat from the kitchen cupboards: granola bars, packages of dehydrated fruit. She shoved them into the half-empty duffel bag.

True moved to the bathroom and grabbed some essentials. She sprinted upstairs to change into something more durable than her sweatpants. The girls held each other's hands on the bed. Hopping on one foot while pulling on jeans, True made it to the window again. She didn't remember opening it, but a breeze made the curtains wave against her cheeks. The last of the jasmine hung in the air.

Through the window screen, a high-pitched whine grew louder, smothering the singing tree, until they all covered their ears with their hands. Bridget's shriek rose above the racket, even as Julianne tucked her under both arms. True slammed the window shut.

"Girls!" Elyse clamored up the stairs and scooped both daughters into her arms, shushing their tears. "It'll be okay. Aunt True's house will stand up. It has special walls. We'll be okay."

True gasped for air and put her hand on the bricks. She didn't know what to do. Tiny stars pinpricked her vision.

"Hey, hey," Elyse said, easing True to the floor. "I need you to take some deep breaths for me." She smiled when True greedily gulped for air. "Good. That's good. Don't need you passing out just yet."

Like a turtle crossing a road, True crawled to the mattress. The girls tucked into her after she lay down. "We'll get through this, kiddos," she whispered into Julianne's hair. "I'll show you how to make dragon scales. And we'll go see movies once a month."

"Will you come to my dance recitals?" Bridget shimmied a hair closer.

"Of course I will."

True buried her nose into Julianne's hair. Bridget kept silent, her eyes bouncing around the room. There was nothing she wouldn't do for these two girls, including smashing down her own fear to keep them safe.

Elyse moved around the room, her steps descending the stairs and retracing their path back up again. She set down the duffle bag near the beds.

True sat up. "Swap with me. I need to get something to block the window."

She looked around her workshop and found some old fence boards she'd always wanted to make into a cute project she'd seen on the internet. Double-checking the secure latch on the roof hatch, True grabbed the boards and returned to the loft.

The trio in the bed watched as True worked on figuring out a way to get the boards to stay. "Well, I can't nail it into the brick."

The drone army returned for a third pass. True glanced at the time on her phone—it'd only been an hour and a half since they'd started. It felt like minutes. She looked down at the now empty valley.

"My phone won't work," True said.

Elyse tried hers again. "Mine won't either."

True propped the boards against the wall. Hopefully, it'd keep glass from flying through the room if the panes broke. She pushed the armchair against them while Julianne turned on the lights, which flickered once, twice, then blinked into darkness. Bridget whimpered.

"We have flashlights," Elyse said, switching one on. Its beam bounced off of the ceiling.

The small engines returned.

"They are going quicker now," Julianne said. She clutched the blankets with both white-knuckled hands.

True nodded. "I'm going to go check the door."

She trotted down the stairs. The bowls on the countertop didn't bother her at all. She closed the window and tried to click the curtain closed with the remote, only to shake her head. No electricity. One more trip to the bathroom, and she shoved money into every pocket she had, tucking some under her clothes.

An open palm slapped the front door three times. Then twice more.

True peeked into the rarely used peephole. Her mother's head looked distorted through the tiny glass. She yanked the door open. "Mom!"

The red apron was tied to her mother's waist, and her hair tumbled out of its bun. Her chest heaved. "He made me come," she panted.

"Come inside." True rebolted the door and looked at her frail mom. When her mom's tears started, True held her. "Let's go upstairs. It's safest there."

"Nana!" Both girls hopped from their cocoon and latched onto the red apron. The elderly woman smoothed their hair in the reflecting light, looking to one daughter, then the other.

"Dad made her come."

Elyse's eyebrow shot up. "He's at home?"

June nodded and clutched her granddaughters closer.

For a fifth time, the drones buzzed the roof. True looked up, following the crack in the ceiling. "They can't fly forever. Their battery life isn't that long."

"You know the weirdest things," Elyse said.

"Trick of the trade."

"Well, I can give you an I.V. and an enema."

"I'll skip, but thank you."

They sat close to one another, wordless until the sixth pass.

"It's going to be over soon," their mother said.

"How do you know, Nana?" Bridget reached out and held her hand.

"Just a feeling. They waited seven days. Maybe it'll be the seventh time around."

True fidgeted. "Mom. Did you see the drones today? They were different."

June looked to her granddaughters. "Nothing to talk about right now. But, I heard the neighbors shouting. Your dad still wouldn't leave, even when I told him."

Elyse grunted.

"I wish he would've come too," True said.

Bridget wiggled onto her Nana's lap. "We can play rock, paper, scissors."

"That's a fine way to pass the time, little love."

The pair slapped their hands in the near dark.

Julianne hovered nearby, engrossed in their hand signals. Her head swiveled to True.

The drones.

"Get on the floor." Elyse's voice wobbled as the engines grew closer. They bunched together, linking arms.

All at once, the army's battle song blasted like it was coming through the walls.

Then nothing.

The heartbeat of silence stretched out for an eternity. The stillness was worse than the noise, as if the entire city was holding its breath. A tick of peace settled just before the window shattered behind the boards. The armchair shoved forward, spilling daylight into the room.

Screaming.

True gathered Bridget and Julianne to Elyse and shielded them as best as she could. Their mom's bony fingers dug into True's elbow as she covered Elyse.

The floor rocked. Even through the mattress, the wood planks rattled True's kneecaps as shockwaves rocked one right after the other. Somewhere below, glass was breaking in a succession of destruction. A shattering symphony.

Chunks of plaster banged into True's back. The powder seeped into her nose and mouth, leaving a chalky taste on her tongue.

Metal screamed in an anguished twist downstairs and True was sure her front door was collapsing. Underneath and above it all, the girls wailed from the middle of the huddle.

They moved and fell to the side with another impact. Collecting themselves again onto the mattress, True caught sight of her mother's bloody hand.

In the workroom, a cacophony of ruin sounded as every last project slammed into the floor or walls.

A huge explosion ripped a gap in the floorboards under the mattress. The entire clan scrambled backwards, reconvening in a cluster near the stairs. Jagged gashes in the mortar allowed more sunlight to emphasize the thick plaster dust.

As a bomb detonated nearby, Bridget yelped again as they were collectively shoved into the wall.

True kissed her sister's forehead. Every sound, every moment heralded their impending deaths. A massive section of the ceiling near the window collapsed, Julianne's dancing box slamming into the floor, vibrations jolting the wood beneath their feet. True closed her burning eyes.

Somewhere near her ribcage, Bridget shook with sobs. True let go of her mother and stroked Bridget's messy braid.

"It stopped," Julianne whispered, then coughed.

The quietness had returned, only to be interrupted by the woeful tune of the singing tree teetering near the gaping hole in the roof.

June's brown eyes were the only color on her white-dusted body when they stood. Elyse clutched her girls. True hacked when she took a deep breath.

Men began shouting outside—enemy soldiers giving orders and calling out as they cleared areas. True shook like a dragon scale on the box. She'd almost saved them.

True held her breath until her lungs burned.

Someone banged on the front door.

When True moved to the stairs, four pairs of hands restrained her.

"No!" Elyse's grip was the strongest. "We can make it to the ladder."

True knew their salvation was downstairs. "Do you trust me?"

"I don't know."

"You trusted my weird, reinforced walls."

"What does that have to do with the army? They'll kill us." Elyse shook her head in tiny movements, clawing at True's arm.

"Let me go. We will be safe. I promise you." The person knocked harder, faster.

Elyse's powdered eyebrows bunched down as she gasped. "I don't understand. I don't know if I want to understand."

True nodded to Julianne and Bridget. "They are all that matters to you. Let me go."

Once released, True picked her way down the teetering stairs. In a moment of thought, she brushed her cheeks clean with the back of her hands before opening the door.

Holoke studied her, his men fanned out in formation behind him. Beyond the small battalion, soldiers climbed the ruins of every leveled building, their calls of "clear" randomly punctuated by single gunshots into the rubble.

"Thank God you're all right." Holoke took a step forward.

True wavered between hugging him and remaining composed. She chose the latter. "Your God-with-a-big-G heard our promise. That's the type of God I could follow."

He smiled and looked over her shoulder. "Is your family inside?"

"Most of them. My father refused to come."

"I am sorry."

"Thank you." Upstairs, Bridget cried. "What now?"

"You are free to go. No one here will stop you and your family. I promise, you're safe."

"Don't look back," True said, before they left the house. She kept her hands over Julianne's eyes and Bridget tucked her head into Elyse's shoulder as the women picked their way through chunks of concrete to spare the girls the death and devastation. Eyes straight ahead, the group walked on the shoulder of the road, toward the trampled valley the army had vacated.

"Look." Bridget sniffed and lifted her finger toward the cliffs.

The red brick walls of True's home stood like a soldier at attention among his fallen comrades. Waving in the breeze, the rope ladder swayed from the fire escape. In the darkened downstairs window, a flashlight burst twice.

Turning back to the asphalt ahead, True pressed her lips together to smother her smile.

The End

Acknowledgements:

*deep breath and try to remember everyone**

Dad & Mom. Thank you for being godly examples. And for letting me read way past my bedtime.

Michael. You've let me do some crazy things. I love you more for it.

Bean & Squish. Always chase your dreams, even when it's hard or they are put on hold. Remember to sing loudly in the car.

Cindy Coloma, Cathy Elliott, and Sarah Sundin. For being a few of the best mentors a gal could ask for.

Rachel Kent. You took a chance on me after being ambushed in an ice cream shop. You answer my weird questions. Best. Agent.Ever!

Joanne Bischof and John Vonhof. You both gave me hope after my spirits were crushed. I don't think this book would be here if you hadn't encouraged me. I will be forever grateful for your kindness.

Hannah Prewett. Remember when we tricked ourselves that first year? Those awful beds? You keep me honest. And you always answer my texts.

The Ever Afters. My favorite people in the sandbox. It's been such an honor to grow with you all. All hail the cast-offs!

My beta readers, especially Rosemary and Elizabeth. Gracias, ladies. Twin introverts, unite!

Rich Bullock. For your editing, help, and infinite indie publishing knowledge.

To those I didn't mention by name. Don't be sad. You know I'm forgetful. Remind me to name a character after you in the next book.

And the last shall be first. To my savior, Jesus Christ, for giving me these stories. May they honor You.

Made in the USA
San Bernardino, CA
14 March 2019